WITCH PLEASE

MAYA DANIELS

VINCI BOOKS

By Maya Daniels

Chronicles of Forbidden Witchery

Resting Witch Face
Pitch a Witch
Witch Please
Payback is a Witch

Vinci Books

vinci-books.com

Published by Vinci Books Ltd in 2025

1

Copyright © Maya Daniels 2023

The author has asserted their moral right to be identified as the author of this work in accordance with the Copyright, Designs and Patents Act 1988. This work is a work of fiction. Names, characters, places and incidents are the product of the author's imagination or are used fictitiously. Any resemblance to actual persons, living or dead, places and incidents is entirely coincidental.

All rights reserved. No part of this publication may be copied, reproduced, distributed, stored in any retrieval system, or transmitted in any form or by any means, including photocopying, recording, or other electronic or mechanical methods, nor used as a source for any form of machine learning including AI datasets, without the prior written permission of the publisher.

The publisher and the author have made every effort to obtain permissions for any third party material used in this book and to comply with copyright law. Any queries in this respect should be brought to the attention of the publisher and any omissions will be corrected in future editions.

A CIP catalogue record for this book is available from the British Library.

Paperback ISBN: 9781036705800

Chapter One

I watched everyone around me with a morbid sort of detachment because all I could offer them was some clumsy commiseration thanks to my miserable existence.

Okay fine, I pitied the fools.

They needed to be included in my wretchedness anyway and what better way to accomplish that than to feel sorry for them.

The voices coming from the book announcing they were the Fates rang like a gong in my mind's ear on repeat and nothing could compare to that insanity. Apparently, who we were created to be was pretty much dead and gone from this world we lived in, as I was told. Women simply weren't as healing, nurturing, and soft as they used to be. Men in return weren't as courageous, honorable, and as strong as they used to be. It's the degradation of a system based on ego and rigid intellectual coldness.

It's the devolution of humanity.

And where humanity went, supernaturals followed, of

course. Far be it from us to stay behind some pathetic humans. 'Am I right?

All of it was happening because we lost the inner values. We slammed the door shut to spirit.

We got lost.

That's what the voices in my head were screaming from the top of their lungs twenty-

four-seven. The bloody bastards!

You must have a reverence for the divine feminine, they told me. You must have a reverence for the divine masculine. You must have a code of honor. Inner power is the ability to maintain that honor which then opens the mystical doorways to the Spirit. And only this can lead you home.

Apparently, only this will allow me to use my ancestral magic which according to my insanity was the answer to everything.

The voices were persistent, I'd give them that.

Good for them.

Not that I had any intention of listening to the nonsense. I personally wanted to find the nearest bar, so I could get plastered.

I was in desperate need of high quality (I still have standards), strong booze.

The one that you'd feel burning down your throat for days after you've recovered from the hangover and the imprint of the toilet seat on your hands from hugging it tightly is long gone.

Call it what you may but getting piss ass drunk for the night and forgetting everything and everyone for just a moment sounded delightful to me. Maybe better than shopping therapy, if I was being honest.

Okay fine, that's a lie. Nothing is better than shopping,

but getting hammered came in second to best in my humble opinion.

I had every intention of making it happen, too.

"Black?" Sissily tucked a hanger with a silky black blouse under her chin. "Or blue?" A second one replaced the first, the indigo kami swaying gently around her torso with the movement.

"Why do they both look familiar?" My eyes narrowed on her face when her expression changed from thoughtful to one of shock with a comical widening of her eyes. She tried to recover quickly; I had to be proud of her for that but there was no way I'd let her get away with it. "Both came from my closet, didn't they?"

"You haven't touched these in at least a year and a half, they were getting depressed and lonely, from being shunned in the deep dark recesses at the back of your closet." My friend muttered defensively, and she wasn't ready to let this go. "If I remember correctly, and these are your words not mine, you wouldn't be seen dead in something so last season." Her peepers rolled to the back of her head playfully and I couldn't stop my lips from curling up.

I was giving her a hard time just to have fun. The woman was wearing additional clothing on her person to cover my clumsy ass every time I needed to replace what I was wearing. I had no right to complain even if she took every piece of fabric I owned. Designer or otherwise.

"And you thought I'd be willing to be seen with you wearing something so last season?" My arched eyebrow was answered with a derisive snort. "I didn't think so."

"I figured I'd at least make an effort, since you are very adamant about going out. I'm sure I'll never hear the end of it if I try to step out of the room in a t-shirt." Tossing both hangers on the armchair with a huff, she threw herself onto the bed next to me. "Why can't we just go grab a couple," she saw my scowl and amended the ridiculous statement immediately. "A few actually, now that I think about it, bottles of wine or gin, and bring them here? We can get perfectly drunk in Pj's, too. No need for fancy clothing or makeup. Get what I mean? It'll be comfy as all hell, as well."

"If I stay in this room for another hour, I'm going to self-combust, Sissily." It was not an exaggeration of the truth, and she knew it. "The longer we mingle, the more I have an urge to jump out of my skin, claw my ears off, or poke out my eyeballs. Can we just go?"

"You sure we will be good to leave the house?" Sissily queried, trying and epically failing to hide the worry creasing the corners of her eyes, she rolled off the bed and stood up. "Friend or not, Alex gives me the heebie-jeebies every time he focuses on me."

"Yeah, he knows we are going to the pub for a drink. He owns the place after all it's not like we can hide on pack lands." Following her example, I stood too and started searching for my shoes while pretending the lightheadedness was not there. "I was very clear that I will either go or his home might blow up like Danika's coven building. You should see how fast he agreed."

"I bet he did." Snickering under her breath as if the alpha was standing on the other side of my closed door, waiting to hear if she would say something bad about him, she was almost gleeful when she turned to face me. "We can totally get anything we want if we use you as a threat like that."

"Oh yeah?" Noticing the heel poking out from under a pile of dirty clothing next to the dresser, I shook my head at her as I bent over to pick it up. "And what would you…"

Whatever else was about to come out of my mouth was forgotten when dizziness made me tip over to the side and my whole-body weight slammed into the drawers of the tall dresser. The few decorations and the group of three vases perched on top of it rattled loudly, one of the glass tubes smacking hard on the wood and rolling off of it to shatter on the parquet floor at my feet. My stomach rolled from the bile that churned inside it as numbness spread through my limbs followed by a cold sweat which drenched my tank top in no time.

"Hazel!" Sissily was next to me so fast I would've flinched when she grabbed me by the shoulders if I could. "Hazel, talk to me girl. What's wrong?"

I must give credit to Sissily. For a tiny little thing the woman was strong. She bodily carried me back to the bed where she dropped me like some poorly chosen prom dress, she regretted buying. All I could do was breathe through my nose and press my lips tight in case the acid burning inside me decided to erupt violently, but I watched her while she frantically turned this way and that not knowing what to do. Suddenly she spun on her heel and rushed to the door that she proceeded to yank open hard enough to make the frame groan.

"Alex!" my friend bellowed from the top of her lungs. The silent house met her shout. "Amber! Hazel needs help!"

As if she used a magic word the emptiness of the home became a cacophony of sound with people calling out to each other and a few pairs of feet came running across the floor in our direction. Remembering the conversation, I had with the alpha a couple of hours earlier I almost laughed. The poor male thinks I'm about to redecorate his home and is probably debating if he should toss me out the window just in case.

"Where is she?"

My heart stopped at the sound of the deep baritone and all the blood drained from my head. My mind was screaming no but there was absolutely nothing I could do to stop the clusterfuck that was about to unfold. To make matters worse, I watched mortified as River rushed to my side and gathered my limp, sweat soaked body in his arms.

"What happened? The pack is taking up positions around the house as a double protection." Blondie looked sharply at my friend who hovered over me like a mother hen, wringing his hands.

"Speak female!"

"Don't you yell at me River Blackman." Sassily hissed at him, getting in his face and if I could, I would've kissed the girl. Good for her telling the jerk off. I mean who died and made him one of the gods? "If I knew do you think I'd be shouting for help like an idiot? One moment she was mocking me about last season's fashion and bent over to pick up her shoe, the next she dropped like a rock pale as a ghost."

"Hazel, can you hear me?" Rough fingers rasped over the skin on my forehead as he brushed hair out of my face. "Does anything hurt? Blink once if you can't talk." Sissily's face popped above me crinkled with worry. "At least she's not bleeding, that's a good thing." River muttered to himself.

"Security is tight around the house. Is she hurt?" Alex rushed into the room filling it up with potent alpha energy strong enough to pebble my skin. "Is she breathing?" His worried face joined my friend above me and all I could do was stare at both of them.

No sound was coming out of me anytime soon. A strange tingling sensation started on my lips and slowly spread all over my face and body, but it did nothing but remind me I was not dead, at least not yet at any rate. At least it wasn't unpleasant or painful; and with my experiences lately everyone was all hellbent on killing me. I was grateful for that.

"Should I call for a healer?" Alex turned his mismatched gaze to River as if blondie held the knowledge of what would help me.

"I think she can hear us but for whatever reason she can't talk." Sissily reached a hand out and yanked on my right eyelid, lifting it up to expose most of my eyeball. In front of Blackman.

The woman was mental.

Lucky for her I couldn't slap her. I made a note to do it as soon as I regained movement to my limbs. The tingling was getting stronger at that point, so with Hecate's help I'd be smacking her any time now. The thought made me giddy with excitement; it also distracted me enough to avoid a panic attack. You'd think I'd be used to this shit by now but no. I was still quaking in my designer shoes every minute of every day expecting to drop where I stood for no reason at all.

It was the story of my life now.

Thank you, stupid magic.

And to think I was begging any gods who listened or the universe to grant me the wish of having power like the rest of my kind. No wonder humans said be careful what you wish for, you just might get it.

The pentagram on the side of my forefinger started burning strong enough that the harsh breath I sucked in sounded like a hiss.

"She's coming around." Sissily took my hand in hers and gave it a reassuring squeeze before dropping it like it bit her. "Oh, dear Hecate, her skin is burning up." Her blue peepers turned accusingly to River. "Why are you sitting there mute, Blackman? You waiting to see if she catches on fire?"

"She's cool to the touch." A line formed between his eyebrows as he searched my face for discomfort was my guess. The fingers of one of his hands glided over my arm raising goosebumps on my skin. "Unless..."

Blessed reprieve came when he took my hand in his, where his skin connected with my burning flesh. The tears which were gathering in the corners of my eyes were gone too and the tingling sensation faded as well. That was my cue to get away from him because it seemed like he knew that he could help remove the pain I was experiencing.

The last thing I needed was to owe Blackman anything.

"I'm okay." I rasped out on a deep breath as soon as my tongue felt less thick in my mouth. "I'm fine." My attempt to push away from River so I can place distance between us, as expected, failed miserably. I only managed to flop around like a fish out of water rubbing myself all over his lap. Speaking of which, "I just need some water." I told no one in particular but they stared at me like I suddenly grew a second head. "... Please?" I added lamely after a long awkward pause raising the pitch of my tone just enough to make it a question.

God forbid anyone mistakes me for a polite individual.

"She's dying." Sissily wailed taking fistfuls of Alex's shirt in a white-knuckled grip.

"Ha, ha. Very funny." Grumbling under my breath, I kept up my attempt to dislodge River. "I've barely eaten anything today so that must be the reason for the dizziness. Nothing a

few burgers and a handful of desserts can't fix."

Alex was already nodding and pulling his phone out of the back pocket of his jeans. Dejectedly, I watched my escape for the night die a sudden death when the alpha ordered a ton of food to be brought up to my room. Any chance of getting plastered went down the drain with it unless I could convince Sissily to go get a few bottles as she earlier suggested. My gaze narrowed on my friend's face, and she returned the favor already reading my expression that I was contemplating something.

In all the scrutiny I was giving my friend, River's hand slipped under my tank top from the wiggling I was doing turning me into a stone statue when I became as stiff as a board. "For Hecate's sake Blackman, you are like a damn octopus. Keep those tentacles to yourself would ya?"

He took mercy on me and released me finally with a maddening smirk on his face. Sissily didn't help matters with the couple of snorts she was trying her best to cover up with a cough. Even Alex was hiding a grin by rubbing a hand over his mouth.

"I'm glad I can amuse all of you." Twisting my lips to show my displeasure, I plopped onto the mattress and blew at the strand of hair that fell over my face. That's when this whole thing took a turn toward a clusterfuck of epic proportions.

"River?" came a soft feminine voice from the open door of my room.

You could hear a pin drop.

We all turned to find a rather attractive blonde with big emerald eyes smiling shyly at Blackman. A sharp pain speared me in the center of the chest that I pretended I didn't notice, and I forced my mouth to stretch into a smile while glancing at my friend. Sissily shook her head sharply to tell me I probably looked hideous, so I dropped the expression immediately.

"I'm sorry, I didn't know you were busy." The pretty blonde blinked at River so seductively even I wanted to go shove my tongue down her throat. "I'll see you later." She turned to leave but as always, I was a glutton for punishment.

Everyone kept their mouth shut, even River. Did I do that as well, you ask?

No.

Have you met me? Of course, I wanted to make him feel as awful as I felt. If I had to suffer, so should he, the insufferable bastard!

"Who's your friend, River?" My chirpy tone made Sissily groan as if in pain.

"I think I'm developing a headache too." My bestie told the alpha who was rubbing his temples and shaking his head at Blackman.

"What?" My innocent question didn't fool anyone, not even me, and it made a muscle spasm in River's jaw.

Seriously. Sometimes you just can't win against people.

Lesson 13: *Everything is fair in love and war, unless you are a witch. It's like a train wreck; you are cringing but can't force yourself to look away.*

I butchered the hell out of everything, and obviously I butchered any chances of love coming my way, too.

Chapter Two

"I don't understand why I can't ask a simple question without it turning into a pack drama." I told Sissily as I stuffed a handful of fries in my mouth. "Isf wuf ouf of pofuftnes." My chipmunk cheeks puffed out as I tried to talk with a mouthful before swallowing the food half chewed in my urgency to argue my case. "It was out of politeness." I repeated in case she misunderstood my food filled sentence earlier as I wiped the grease from my mouth with the back of my hand.

According to Alex and Sissily, I was being an ass and making River's life miserable. To which I disagreed wholeheartedly. "I can be polite you know. What?" She was about to roll her eyes I could feel it, but my glare made her think better of it. "I can."

"You?" Sissily leaned back and looked at me up and down before nodding thoughtfully. "You can totally be polite and very nice." My smile full of gratitude was as premature as Mike's ejaculation according to the stories my bestie had told me. "You just chose to be rude."

Well, she wasn't wrong about that. I did choose to be rude, but I had my reasons for that, damn it.

"Anywhoooo," picking the pickle out of my burger I slapped it on the plate with disgust. A shiver ran up and down my spine as I fished between the buns for more of the yucky things. "I wasn't trying to be rude or mean. I was honestly curious about who the bombshell was. Weren't you?"

The mumble coming out of my bestie was the buzzing of a mosquito and it abruptly cut off when my hand froze with my fingers in the burger up to the second knuckle and my eyes narrowed dangerously on her face.

"I'm sorry, what?" It was so unusual to watch Sissily squirm that I almost dropped the burger in my lap.

"I said," on a deep exhale, she deflated like a balloon looking all dejected and shit. "I've seen him talking to her a few times while you were recovering from the last blood loss. I was hoping to avoid you seeing it though."

"Why?" recovering my food I took a huge bite and chewed thoughtfully while watching her like a hawk. "You think I care who River talks to?" Genuinely puzzled, I finally asked when I swallowed the bite.

"You don't?" Sissily challenged with one eyebrow arrowed up.

No was on the tip of my tongue but since my bestie rarely sassed me about males, I took a deep breath and examined my thoughts and feelings on the matter. Life was crappy as it was without taking things too seriously; so, we both acted immature on most days to offset the stress we faced. Occasionally though we had to be adults.

"I am a hot-blooded female, Sissily. It would be a lie if I said I don't think about jumping Blackman's bones at least three times a day. I have a vagina." Both eyebrows raised, I pointed to my crotch in case she didn't know where the organ was located. "That being said I rather he stays away from me as far as possible; so, him talking to other females is a good thing."

There. I could be an adult. Don't look at me like that! I could!

Neither Sissily, nor I for that matter believed a word coming out of my mouth.

"I can always zap her and burn her hair to a crisp." Sissily offered conversationally while plucking layers of flaky dough from the croissant she's been gnawing on the last twenty minutes. "No one looks good with a typhus hairstyle. I bet she won't look good then."

I snorted despite myself.

"You're so stupid."

"Genius you mean?"

"That, too." Returning her smile, I continued eating because I really hated the fact I couldn't get out of the damn room and get plastered because of dizziness from lack of nourishment. With everything going on, I would forget to eat on most days unless someone reminds me. Amber was mothering the hell out of me but with the increase of attacks on pack lands the poor female could barely remember her own name.

Howls sounded from outside, loud enough to be heard crystal clear in my room. Another reminder that thanks to me no one was safe. And here I was dwelling on River's love life instead of facing my own crap. As if sensing the direction of my thoughts, or maybe my faraway gaze aimed at the window was an indication, Sissily reassuringly squeezed my arm.

"We will figure things out eventually." She muttered like she was scared to say it too loud and tempt fate.

Speaking of which...

"What do you suppose it means?" my bestie knew exactly who I was referring to without me voicing it. "It could be a demonic trick."

I still refused to accept the fact that the cursed book was somehow a portal for communicating with the Fates. The way the demons have been attacking every chance they get and recruiting the rest of the supernaturals, I wouldn't put it pass them to try trickery. It was their very nature after all. No one could blame a snake for biting them. It's a snake, it's what they do.

Same with demons.

Unless they try to eat your designer shirt. That shit is simply unheard of.

Sissily lifted her face and made a loud sniffing sound. My frown made her grin at me like a fiend. "I can smell something burning. You are trying to use your brain, huh? Don't think too hard it'll short circuit."

I kicked at her, or at least I tried halfheartedly to kick her, I should say. Her giggle was short-lived and cut off when the second set of howls nearly shook the house with its intensity. After a few seconds of staring at each other owlishly, we scrambled off the bed and raced toward the curtain covered window.

Parting the thick fabric slightly, I did my best to see in the pitch black what was going on with one eye. Sissily was doing the same on the other side, her breath seesawing in the silence of the room but I doubt she was having any better luck. It seemed that someone plunged the grounds around the large home into darkness and only an occasional eerie glow of predatory eyes broke it. Luckily those I saw all belonged to the wolves.

"Something is going on out there." Sissily said, her voice trembling from the adrenaline I too was experiencing.

"You think?" craning my neck and pressing my forehead harder to the glass where my nose was squished sideways, I snorted at her. "No shit, Sherlock." My breath fogged up the window, and I missed if it was a wolf looking up at where we were or if it was something else.

"You're such a jerk." My bestie groused, pouting at me from the other side of the window when I looked her way.

"I'm going." Not allowing her time to process what I said, I rushed around the room and hurriedly stabbed my feet into the flattest boots I could find. They ended up having a two-inch heel but better than a stiletto, I guess.

"Like I thought you'd do something else, Hazel. You do remember I've known you since we were kids, right?"

A shrill scream rattled the windows, and I made a mad dash toward it yanking on the curtain without a second thought. We were beyond the point of hiding. Whoever was out there didn't care to stay hidden anymore, so I didn't see why I should be hiding either. After all, I was pretty sure they were here for me. Sissily stepped up next to me as we gazed down into the darkness of the back yard.

A shadow slithered between two shrubs, their leaves rusting from the disturbance, but they were too fast for my eyes to track. A few of the clouds parted at that moment thankfully allowing the partial moon to illuminate the yard long enough that I was able to identify the usurper. My heart skipped a beat before stuttering into a rapid-fire rhythm.

"Mazzikin." Sissily and I said at the same time as we locked gazes.

Mazzikin is not a specific type of demon from Hell

specifically, but rather they are a broad classification of a range of evil spirits in the same way we see demons. They are the cheeky little blighters of the demon hierarchy, maddeningly irritating and hard to get a hold of. They are as pesky as the imps who are permanently armed with the spanners that so often get thrown into the works but more vicious when it comes to harming supernaturals. In short, Mazzikin are mean little critters, or invisible types of demons, who cause everyday stressors and tribulations for humans. The problem was, wherever these little buggers showed up, much bigger problems followed for those like me.

There was only one way to get rid of the Mazzikin and luckily for the pack, Danika being her typical self and tormenting me with useless knowledge was about to pay off big time.

"Let's go." I snatched my bestie by the hand and yanked her along with me through the door and out into the hallway. It was as empty as a tomb which was expected with all the fighting and howling going on outside. "I know what to do."

"You do?" Sissily panted as we took the stairway down two stairs at a time.

Yes, I do." Gasping for air, as well, I sped up. "Mazzikin are spirits, Sissily. What's the easiest way to get rid of them from this plane of existence? Think."

"Hazel! I could kiss you right now." She squealed and redoubled her efforts to get downstairs before me now that she knew what we should do to end the nightmare before someone gets seriously hurt. "Remember though, if Danika asks, we know nothing."

"I'd die before I say a word." I told her solemnly. "We don't need additional things for her to hold over our heads."

The very thought of my grandmother had my blood

boiling, but I pushed it down in order to focus on what we had to do. Reaching the front double doors, I took a hold of the ornate knobs and yanked both open at the same time just as Sissily breezed past me and skidded to a stop within a few feet.

Shifters raced around on four and two legs, shouts and howls echoing in the night. My heart stuttered when I noticed the flickering images of the shades start gathering closer to where the two of us joined the skirmish. I knew they were sent here for me even without the obvious signs.

"We should start now…" Sissily was saying but I waved a hand at her to cut her off and pointed at the cluster of shrubs to the left where two wolves were snapping their jaws at one of the Mazzikin.

"We should wait a little just to be jerks." My grin made her glare at me. "What? He is a know it all, isn't he?" We watched River dance around the shade, his magic passing through it without making a scratch. "This will teach him a lesson."

Dark eyes locked on my gloating face and narrowed with suspicion. I wondered for a split second if he heard me and that's why he didn't rush to play my guardian, but every thought left the moment a few of the demons beelined for Sissily.

All the blood drained from my head when I realized she was looking at me over her shoulder and didn't see them coming. She was a few feet ahead of me, so they were much closer to her, and I had no chance of reaching her before they did.

"Duck!" My scream had her dropping like a rock, face first onto the concrete path. Blondie was yelling something too, but I blocked him out completely. "Roll!"

My feet were already moving when Sissily rolled toward

me avoiding one of the shades that dove for the spot where she prostrated herself. Sprinting, I bent down as I reached my friend and snatched her up by the arm. She twisted easily, more from years of sparring together than intuition or anything else and pushed herself off of the ground. My momentum helped us both keep our balance and we raced for the line of trees where we could find shelter for a few seconds.

Many howls sounded around us pebbling my skin.

Fear clawed at my insides, guilt drilling a hole in my gut. My petty nature almost cost Sissily her sanity. If any of the Mazzikin possesses a witch, she or he would lose their mind. There was no returning from that.

As we reached the few trees, I slammed my back onto one of the trunks pulling Sissily with me. We both gasped loudly, sucking in air for our starved lungs more out of panic than for being out of shape. Although that damn burger was trying to come up a couple of times since I left the safety of my room.

"Ready?" I panted. "We gotta do it now."

She just nodded spastically while blowing air through her nostrils like a bull.

"*Exorcizamus te, omnis…*" a coughing fit had me doubling over and I almost lost the food I stuffed in my mouth earlier all over the leaf covered ground.

"Hazel!" River's shout had my heart punching the roof of my mouth and without turning to see where he was yelling from, I dropped on the ground pulling Sissily with me.

The short hairs on the back of my neck lifted to attention when I felt the soft tickling breeze from the shade that missed me by a hair.

"Sissily?" My gasp was followed by spitting out leaves that filled my mouth when I faceplanted.

"Start." Anger colored her tone, and she squeezed my hand hard enough to grind my bones. I knew exactly how she felt because I was starting to get pissy, too.

"Exorcizamus te, omnis immundus spiritus, omnis satanica potestas, omnis incursio infernalis adversarii, omnis legio, omnis congregatio et secta diabolica."

Our voices rose with each word but as we finished the chant, oppressive silence formed a vacuum between my ears. Sissily and I looked at each other, both of us wide-eyed and covered in dirt. I could see clear as day the doubt written all over her face if we did this right or if we miscalculated the situation completely.

You could hear a pin drop.

And that's when the shrieks started loud enough to make my ears bleed.

Cursed demons and their penchant for draining the blood from my body.

Chapter Three

Rough hands grabbed both of my shoulders and jerked me upright hard enough my forehead smacked into someone's chest. No. Not someone. Blackman loomed over me, his face set in a harsh determined expression. His mouth was moving but I couldn't hear anything from the whistling sound thundering in my ears so I just slapped at his grabby hands weakly hoping he would release me and go away.

He didn't.

All the energy I had while adrenaline was rushing through my veins drained the moment the Mazzikin started shrieking. It felt like someone shoved me inside a washing machine and put me on spin for an hour. Everything hurt.

Ignoring blondie, I turned my head in search of Sissily and found her pressing both of her ears with her hands while bright red blood trickled between her fingers down her neck. With how pale River looked while he shook me, I guessed I didn't look any better either. I could feel the warm blood gliding over my clammy skin and drenching my tank top.

"Hazel?" speech finally penetrated the thudding in my ears, and River sounded like he was calling my name from underwater. "Can you hear me? Where are you hurt?"

Summoning all the strength I could, I glared at him, but he was unperturbed.

"Please talk to me." Blondie ran his hands over my shoulders down my arms and up as if that would improve my ability to speak. Quite the opposite really but I'd die before I admit that to him.

"I've never been better." My rasp was followed by a forced smile, and I cringed when I saw the reflection of my bloodied teeth in his expanded irises. His forehead wrinkled as if I spoke in tongues, so I turned away from him. I had more important things to do than worry about River.

"Well, that didn't go as planned, huh?" I muttered to my best friend who clawed her way closer to me. "Can you hear?"

Sissily nodded, wincing from the movement, and then proceeded to stare at her bloodied fingers with outer terror. "You?" A coughing fit racked her frame when she attempted to speak.

"I'm great." My friend gave me a worried look when I answered her in a cheerful tone. "I bleed all over the place on regular basis. This is my norm now."

"Did she hit her head?" River asked Sissily to which she answered with a shrug. Both ignored my unimpressed stare. "What were you two doing?" He had to raise his voice because the shrieking was going up in volume by the second.

"We thought we could banish the Mazzikin." Sissily waved a hand at the flickering spirits zooming around us in a zig zag fashion. "They should've gone back to their realm, but something is wrong."

"You think?" River snapped at her angrily and my heart picked up speed. "What gave it away that something is wrong? The way demons used blood magic last time we had to fight our way out of the coven building or...?"

"I'd tread very carefully with how you speak to her, Blackman." Pushing off the leaf-covered ground I got up on my knees forgetting all about the pounding headache doing its best to crack open my skull. "It'll be such a shame for someone to accidentally turn you into an overcooked shish kebab."

"That was reckless, Miss Byrne." The condescending tone he used made me want to punch him in the nose.

"You think?" I barked at him fed up with the lectures. As if I couldn't see that I messed up. "You're still here so that can't be what made my recklessness obvious. What gave it away? Do tell me so I don't repeat that mistake again."

We glared at each other until Sissily tugged on my arm like a toddler trying to get the parents' attention. The constant screaming from the Mazzikin was driving me nuts and wasn't helping matters either. A second later I realized what my friend was warning me about.

"Hazel?" Alex stepped in between the trees; his chest bare as he yanked the sweats up his hips.

"She's fine." River squeezed between his teeth; you'd think I committed the greatest offense by being unharmed.

"Do I want to know?" The alpha cocked an eyebrow at Sissily who was still sitting on the ground in front of me.

"Nope." She didn't even look up, methodically cleaning up the blood from her skin with a handful of leaves. Her ponytail shifted to the side of her head in our one on one with the Mazzikin and a small twig with a few leaves was sticking out of it as if she was an Indian chief.

I plucked it out of her hair, ripping out a few strands along with it.

"Thanks." She hissed at me baring her teeth.

"Don't mention it." I bared mine like a fiend.

"Ladies, ladies." Alex shuffled closer both his hands raised to the side in a placating gesture. His tone was hesitant as if he couldn't believe his own ears that he was talking like that. It sounded alarms in my head immediately. "Let's not argue with ourselves. Someone needs to stop all this screaming before we turn on each other. My pack is getting agitated from the high-pitched tones."

That's when I noticed we were acting aggressively toward each other as well. Well, more so than normal. I don't need demons to want to sock River in his smug handsome face. He does have a very punchable one, and it wasn't Maybelline for sure. He was born with it.

"The demons should've been gone by now." I told the alpha as I took hold of Sissily's arm and pulled her up on her feet. "We used an exorcism chant that is infallible. There is something wrong with this whole thing." Jabbing both hands on my hips I looked around at the erratic spirits in confusion. "I don't get it."

"Danika Byrne has used the same banishing to send demonic forces back to Hell. It always works." Sissily told the two males as if I needed Danika's reference to prove I was telling them the truth.

I was ready to argue that point too when I caught myself and clamped my mouth shut. Whatever it was that the Mazzikin were doing it was making us all aggressive. And River, Sissily and I were standing between a bunch of trees with an entire pack of shifters running around on four legs. Just as the thought occurred to me, I heard the first growl from behind me.

"How fast can you two get to the house?" I asked airily, my gaze jumping from Sissily's face to River's. Cold sweat trickled between my shoulder blades when both of them frowned as if debating my sanity.

Not that we couldn't fight our way out of the situation. I would bet my life that my friend and Blondie didn't want to fight the pack as much as I didn't. Alex was dealing with attacks and his mate and child were taken because he was protecting me. There was no way any of us would fight or harm his pack if we could help it. It was time to scram while we still had control over our actions.

"The Mazzikin are making the wolves aggressive, they can't control themselves." The widening of their eyes in realization would've been comical if we were not in imminent danger. "Last one inside buys dinner."

Alex barked out a surprised laugh when I bolted by him, my shoulder clipping his chest as I passed. Good thing I didn't dislocate it, the male was built like a tank. Adrenaline surged through me as I pumped my arms, giving it my all to reach the open blackened doors of the house. We must've left them open when we rushed to help the pack fight off the Mazzikin. Lot of good that did now that we had to run back inside so we don't end up ripped to shreds if we refuse to fight the wolves.

River and Sissily were right behind me, because when it came to saving my own ass, I turned into lightning even on two-inch heels. We would've made it, too.

I should've known Ace was lurking nearby, however. The male never learned to take care of himself first before looking out for me especially after his alpha announced the pack oversaw my protection. Ace somehow took it personally. My guess was he didn't like that I tricked him to take me off pack lands and almost got myself killed. If I didn't know he was a wolf though, I could've sworn he was a mule. Stubborn to boot. Disheveled, half naked and scratched up he was grinding his molars fighting whatever horror the high tones of the Mazzikin's shrieks did to his animal; tendons were standing out on his neck and his knuckles were turning white while he fisted his hands.

"Get out of my way!" I shouted, not slowing down a bit. "Go, go, go!" I emphasized each "go" by stabbing my finger toward the beckoning front doors.

Ace glared at me, a muscle twitching in his jaw but he didn't move. If I wasn't freaking out, I would've thought it strange that he didn't acknowledge me at all but at the time my brain had a one-track mind. Get inside and away from the wolves. Plus, Blackman was breathing down my neck. He was so close behind me I could feel the heat of his body blasting my skin. Sissily's harsh breathing spurred me on too.

As we neared the shifter, I did the only thing I could think of. I lowered my head and charged him like a raging bull, my magic perking up at the prospect of a fight added a bit of speed as well. Ace shifted slightly spreading his legs a bit more to better balance his weight. I clenched my teeth and plowed right into the center of his chest shoulder first like some football linebacker. I am not sure who was more surprised me, River, or Ace, as I lifted the shifter off his feet and out with a satisfying grunt. A whoosh of air exploded from him that had me grinning from ear to ear like a fool.

"Punch him or move before I blast him unconscious." Sissily huffed from behind me.

"I'm trying not to—"

Ace squeezed my side so hard with his arm around my waist, I thought for sure a kidney would burst or something would break in half if he kept pressing any harder. What was I going to do? Punch Ace? A werewolf as big as the entire friggin' house? "You two go ahead, I'll follow shortly." I panted as loud as I could.

"I don't think so." River growled from right next to me. The next thing I knew, Ace's arm was gone and I was airborne, sailing over a few concrete stairs right toward the double doors. Which, by some bad luck, were now closed. Grunts, and shouts sounded behind me as Blondie continued punching Ace like the shifter was his personal punching bag. Unfortunately, I couldn't even turn around to see what was going on because I had just enough time to hug my head with both arms before I hit the now closed doors made of solid wood at full speed. Pain exploded in my neck when the impact nailed my head and back toward my shoulders, you'd think I was a turtle trying to hide in my shell.

A silent scream lodged in my throat as everything from the top of my head to the middle of my back numbed from excruciating pain that made my body throb like one giant ball of agony.

"You.... are...heavy." Sissily huffed and puffed as she hooked both arms under my shoulders and dragged me over the threshold without stopping for a breath. "Maybe ease up on the burgers and try more greens, yeah?"

My groan of misery wasn't enough for her to give me a break and not lecture me on my food choices, so I just clenched my jaw and pushed with my feet to help her out instead of pointing out she was getting thicker around the waist as well. Hiding to stay alive was wreaking havoc on our figures.

"Get River." The moment my feet were over the threshold I slapped at Sissily's hands. "They'll kill each other."

"Blackman, Hazel is not breathing!" Sissily cupped her hands around her mouth and shouted from the top of her lungs.

"What in Hecate's name are you doing?" recoiling from her I gaped at my friend.

"Where is she?" River materialized in the doorway out of thin air, his hair sticking out in every direction, eyes wild.

"Getting River inside as you asked." Sissily answered me calmly, as she yanked Blondie further inside and slamming the doors shut in Ace's furious, bloodied face. "Now what?"

Chapter Four

I found my wrinkled dirty clothing fascinating in my attempts to avoid looking at River while Sissily cast a spell to hold the doors closed no matter what. The pigeon on the other hand stared at me so intently I could feel heat on the side of my face from it. I was also imagining all the ways I was going to strangle Sissily for being such a jackass. Hecate knows what she was thinking making crazy comments like that. Blackman had an agenda behind offering his protection to me and babysitting my ass. He sure as hell wasn't doing it from the goodness of his heart or goddess forbid because he cared.

My snort had my best friend cocking an eyebrow at me.

I ignored her, too.

"The Mazzikin are not acting like themselves." I told the parquet floor because I refused to make eye contact with either of them. "The pack is reacting to their screams, and we will not under any circumstances harm any wolf. I hope I'm making myself clear."

"Or what?" Sissily snarked. "You gonna spank me?"

"Do you want to hurt any of Alex's pack?" pain was blooming at the back of my neck and spreading over my shoulders. I wanted to puke, and I wasn't in the mood for sass.

"No." taken aback she even physically jerked back.

"Then what's the problem?" With a sigh I scrubbed a hand over my face, smudged dirt all over my skin, and my mouth twisted in disgust when I saw blood, soil and who knows what else on my palm. "And what's wrong with him?" I jabbed my thumb in the direction of River.

"What made you think exorcism would work on the Mazzikin?" Blackman seethed having clearly decided on using the wrong approach. That was a bad call on his part. He was using his accusatory tone while I was already in a pissy mood. I had to wonder if he had been dropped on his head repeatedly as a child.

"Sheesh, I don't know? Maybe the fact that it's the only sure way to get rid of them?" I challenged him slapping my hands on my hips and turning to fully face him. "Why? Did I mess up the nothing you were doing? Sorry, it was not intentional."

"Guys, guys." Sissily waved her hands like that will calm me down. It just made me grind my teeth harder. "Can we not argue with each other? Obviously, something else is going on here." Blowing out a deep breath she glanced at River from the corner of her eye. "We were not thinking; all we wanted was to send them away before they hurt someone." Her forefinger pointed subtly at his legs, and she twirled it.

I frowned at that. River did too for that matter, but she repeated the gesture and delicately cleared her throat. The demons kept shrieking outside and although the sound was somewhat muffled inside the house it was still giving me a headache. I couldn't think straight to save my life.

All confused and trying not to look like a perv, I flicked my gaze at River's lower body but couldn't see what she was getting at. Well, until his head bent down and stayed like that longer than a second before he reached down to zip up his pants like it was the most natural thing in the world to do. Because we unzip the zippers when fighting demons. All the blood rushed to my head, and it developed a heartbeat between my temples.

"Maybe you would've tried something more effective than exorcism if you had circulation to your brain at the time, Blackman. When all your blood travels to your dick, it's hard to think I'm guessing.

Sissily groaned as if pained but I was on a rampage and had no intention of stopping. I knew I should, but I couldn't.

"We didn't mean to inconvenience you while you were getting your dick wet." I told Blondie all haughtily; I almost sounded like Danika. That should've been my cue to shut my trap, but I kept going. "I'll make sure to remind the demons to time their attacks more conveniently. After all, they should know we can't fight properly with blue balls or pointed erections all over the place".

"Feel free to take care of my erection anytime you want, Hazel, so no one else has to do it." Blackman glared at me like it was my fault his zipper was open. "As a matter of fact, how about you do it now?" his hand went to the zipper, and he yanked it down making the pulse pound in my ears.

I saw red.

"That's rude. My dad won't be happy that you talk to Hazel like that, River." A tiny voice cut off my rage like a bucket of ice-cold water was dumped on my head. Sharp pain zapped me when my head jerked sharply towards Jack who was crouched on the bottom step of the stairway but naked and looking at us wide eyed.

"Jack!" Sissily rushed toward the kid tugging the t-shirt over her head. I would have to remind her that she wasn't wearing additional clothing just for me. "Why are you here buddy?"

It felt horrible to know the young boy heard me acting like a dumbass, but I couldn't turn back time. While my best friend was pulling her t-shirt over the kid's head, I skirted around Blackman wider than was necessary and joined them on the stairs. As soon as my butt touched the ground Jack wiggled away from Sissily and climbed in my lap.

"Why you naked kiddo?" wrapping my arms around him I squeezed him tight until he squealed. "Amber will be upset, you know that."

"She told me to stay in my room." The kid pouted and mumbled in my neck as he got comfy, while stretching his legs so they could be in Sissily's lap when she sat next to me.

Something hit the front door with a loud bang. Jack jumped in my arms, his heart hammering against his chest and we looked at each other with my bestie as I hugged him tighter. We had no idea how long the spell would keep the wolves out of the house. The problem was we had no idea what to do and I knew using my magic was the worst idea ever. Hoping the Mazzikin would simply go away was too much to ask.

"But you didn't listen, huh?" River ruffled the kid's hair as he shuffled closer, placing himself between us and the doors. A lot of good that would do but it was better than nothing plus he chose to be an adult and cut off our argument. "You run around parading your little tic-tac size weaner again." The typical banter between these two always started like that.

Jack's head jerked up and he stared at me waiting for permission. Sissily was already shaking her head when I nodded at the kid. His grin of triumph was blinding in its intensity.

"That's why your breath smells so good, River." The boy told Blackman proudly, puffing up his tiny chest and baring his teeth in a gloating smile.

River, choked on air while I had to bite my lips, so I didn't burst out laughing. Even Sissily was snorting under her breath. She didn't want anyone to think she encouraged the boy to listen to me if she full on laughed. As you could guess, it wasn't the first time Blackman made tic-tac jokes with the kid since Jack had the propensity to get out of his clothing and run around naked every chance he had, so I might've helped him out a bit with his comeback. The timing for him talking back to Blackman though was immaculate. Not even I could predict the perfection of the situation.

"You shouldn't listen to Hazel, Jack." Sissily wanted to sound stern, instead she sounded choked up because she was trying not to giggle. "She's going to get into a lot of trouble when your mom hears her."

"No, she won't." he jutted up his little chin daring her to tell him otherwise. "I won't tell on her and if you do, I'll say you're lying." I was so proud of the kiddo and gave him an affectionate squeeze. Although I lacked maternal instincts, the tiny shifter was slowly becoming one of my favorite people.

When he didn't go anywhere near my closet I mean. I was working on allowing people get close to me, but not that close.

Another bang sounded at the doors, this one bowing the wood inward hard enough we heard it groan and crack. All humor evaporated, although we all put our bickering aside for Jack's sake since we had no idea what to do next apart from wait it out, I guess. The poor kid was trembling in my arms, his little fingers digging into my skin and a familiar urge to protect him surged through me strong enough it almost doubled me over.

"Oh, shit." Sissily gasped before slapping a hand over her mouth. "Crap, I meant crap." She mumbled staring wide-eyed at my glowing skin. I lit up like a Christmas tree. "No! Sheesh. Yes, that's the word I was looking for. Sheesh."

My friend was blubbering because she was freaking out. Nothing good came out when I turned into a Fourth of July show, and I had Jack in my arms at the time. Another bang at the doors had River yanking the kid away from me. River folded Jack close into his body to protect him. Jack immediately started wiggling to get away from him. That was the worst decision of the night, and that's including the exorcism attempt Sissily, and I did.

"Let me go!" Jack was immediately screaming as loud as the damn Mazzikin. "Hazel! Help me! Hazel!"

A howl of an alpha rattled all the windows in the house.

"We need to get out of here. Now!" the last thing we needed was a pissed off alpha not in charge of his mind.

Yanking Jack back into my arms I took the stairs two at a time while he wrapped his little skinny legs around my waist. Sissily was right behind me, smart enough to save her own life and not worry about Blackman. Blondie fortunately, has wings and can take care of himself.

The front door crashed and burst inward into a million pieces. A half-shifted Alex filled up the doorway murder written all over his face. Ace was shoulder to shoulder with him.

"I'd fly if I were you, River!" My shout was followed with a burst of feathers from Blackman's back.

"Oh shit!" Jack repeated proudly, copying what Sissily said earlier with the exact intonation. If I wasn't so afraid that the three of us were about to die, I would've laughed.

Chapter Five

My room was a poor excuse for a shelter from a pissed off Alex, but it had to do in a pinch. Sissily slammed the door shut and pressed her back to it as if that would stop him from coming after his son who was giggling in my arms. At least the kid had fun if nothing else. Hysterical laughter bubbled up my throat, but I swallowed it down.

"We need to get out of here before they get past Blackman." Dropping Jack on top of my bed with a bounce and an excited squeal from him, I rushed to the dresser so I could grab the few daggers I had stashed in my underwear drawer. Very inventive I know but it worked obviously since no one had found them so far. They were where I left them, and I sheathed each at the small of my back. Hecate help me! I hoped I never had to use them against anyone in the pack. They risked their lives to keep me safe and it was my fault this was happening to them with the damn spirits.

"I want my mommy." Jack pouted at me when I turned to check on him.

"You stay right here, and I'll go get Amber, okay?"

forcing a smile I glared at Sissily in case she decided to correct me in my lie. Her cocked eyebrow said, 'And if I do call you out what are you going to do about it?' but she wisely stayed out of it.

"I'm going to come, too, Hazel." The boy started wiggling in his attempt to jump off the high mattress and my heartrate picked up pace.

"No!" even I flinched at my tone. "It's not safe out there, Jack." It took everything in me to keep my voice soft when all I wanted to do was scream. "You stay here, and your mom will come before you know it. But we must go find her first."

"No, I want to go, too." He started arguing and I was about to yell at the poor kid.

"You know what?" Sissily finally broke her vow of silence and took one step away from the door, one hand stretched out toward the boy. "You are staying right here." A rope of fire erupted from her fingertips, and it formed a circle around Jack an inch above the covers on my bed. "Let's go. Woman."

"Are you kidding me?" Outraged, I gaped at her while Jack started shrieking louder than the Mazzikin demons outside. "We can't pin this on Blackman, so you better have a good reason for it. What in Hecate's name possessed you?"

"He can't leave the room like this, and we need him safe." My friend waved me off nonchalantly as if this was what we did to people on a daily basis. "We must do something to fix the spell we cast, and we can't stay here with everyone out of their mind. If we take him with us, the pack will follow. So…"

She had a very good point, and I clamped my mouth shut with all the complaints I had sitting on the tip of my tongue. "Alex might be pissed off now, but he will thank us later when he comes to his senses, you are right." I agreed begrudgingly with her.

It was almost thirty minutes or more since we attempted the exorcism but neither did the demons vanish; nor did they calm down enough to stop screaming. We were not shifters, but even we were ready to jump out of our skins from the noise which was building like pressure behind my eyeballs.

"I need to either find Leviathan or we need to go drop in on Destin. That bloodsucker better start singing about who we need to confront so we can put an end to this nonsense." That was as far as I would go to agree with her on the we need to go plan. Something inside me screamed that I should stay in my room and not step toe out the door.

No toes would be touching the floor outside if they were covered though.

One look at my shoes, however, told me I needed to change them. I love a chunky heel as much as any woman with a style, but they are useless around vamps if we did end up in the lair of the master vampire. My stiletto boots on the other hand were as sexy as they were deadly. Destin wouldn't know what hit him if we did end up seeing him when he got ready to have his breakfast.

"We will have better luck visiting a vampire nest during the daytime." Sissily rolled her eyes when she saw me switching shoes.

I ignored her.

"Okay fine, we will go and see where Levi is hiding these days…" the door burst open so hard it swung hard into the opposite wall with a crash.

Thankfully, I had enough control not to release the

dagger pinched between my fingers when I whirled to see who forced their way into my room.

Shirtless, River ducked and rolled all over my floor like some communist gymnast from Mother Russia, dressed in nothing but speedos with his blonde locks tussled from the wind. Don't ask me how I knew what those gymnasts looked like. I have TikTok like all the humans and watched dumb shit while stuck in my room, so I could keep my head attached to my shoulders.

Sissily, unlike me, was trigger happy though, so while I stopped myself from making Blackman an anthill or a pile of ash, she threw fire at him and almost turned him into a roasted pigeon wearing a diaper. His fast reflexes were his only saving grace. Even I could admit that it would've been a shame to mar his perfect looks.

On a closer inspection after he twisted away from the fireball and popped up off the floor like Jack in a box, I realized he was not actually wearing speedos. Those were his pants shredded all the way to his hips by sharp teeth. By the looks of it, wolves might've tried to gnaw on his legs, and they ended up with mouthful of fabric instead. The only cloth left was just enough to cover his rounded buttocks and his groin. It was so absurd, a laugh burst out of me that not even my hand covering my mouth could stop.

"It's hilarious, I know." Blondie deadpanned unimpressed by my ability to find humor in the situation.

"Oops." Sissily gasped, a horrified expression twisting her features. "Sorry, River."

"Don't mention it." He waved off her concern. "We don't have much time; we have to go."

"Go where?" Although that was our plan too, I sounded suspicious of his actions when the question popped out of my mouth. Sissily looked as if she was going to make a comment about it, but she changed her mind immediately and pressed her mouth in a firm line that whitened her skin at the corner of her lips.

Smart woman.

"Anywhere but here." River combed his hair with his fingers more out of agitation than the need he had to fix the mad scientist vibe he had going on. It was written clearly in the tense set of his jaw and the narrowing of his eyes.

At least Jack stopped screaming. Instead of attempting to burst my ear drums he was trying to touch the flames dancing in a circle around him with yelps every time they licked at his finger.

"If you are serious about trying to find Leviathan now, I think it'd be best to go to his domain first." Sissily threw out casually after delicately clearing her throat. You'd think Blackman was part of the conversation from the get-go the way she included him, and he slid into it without blinking an eye, nodding and centering his full attention on her. "I've never been there personally but I've heard it's not hard to gain access." Her fingers flicked at some invisible lint on her shirt before she lifted her gaze and met mine levelly.

"You mean gain access to Hell?" making sure I understood her correctly my eyebrows hit my hairline when she nodded as if entering Hell and knowing the location to its gates was a common occurrence.

"I'm not disagreeing that it's a good idea but hear me out first before telling me I'm a naysayer." Bending down I finished putting my shoes on so I could buy myself some time to think. "Jack stop touching those flames before you burn your fingers for real." My mouth twisted in distaste when I heard my tone. I sounded like a human. I had the misfortune to come across a few of those soccer moms in my life and let me tell you, they are an entirely different species of humans. I'd leave it at that.

"She's not getting any maternal instincts." My best friend explained to Blackman who must've looked puzzled by my comment. "She just doesn't want to upset Amber or Alex after everything they've done for her. It has nothing to do with the safety of the kid."

Rising up to my full height I nodded at Blondie to confirm the statement. Otherwise, who knew what weird notions he would get into his head.

"What she said." My forefinger stabbed the air toward Sissily's face for emphasis. "The fact that we have Mazzikin around that cannot be sent back to Hell tells me we need to act fast. Each day things are getting worse and although Danika wants me tucked in safe, I think if Muhammed can't go to the mountain, then the mountain will go to Muhammed."

"She's learning human metaphors through apps." Sissily was having a separate conversation with Blackman.

Blondie nodded thoughtfully which irked me to no end. "Which means?"

"She is agreeing that we need to go visit Hell." My bestie translated for him totally missing my glare that could've melted her face if my powers decided to gift me mental strength to inflict physical harm.

Both looked at me with expectant expressions on their faces like I was a monkey in a Zoo about to perform some trick.

"I feel like a cockroach in a chicken fight." I told them. Sissily shrugged a shoulder when Blackman turned to her for another translation. If they want to be jerks, I could get creative with the metaphors. "We should go now before either the Mazzikin cause great harm to the pack or Alex storms in here and kill us all. I think the demons will follow us if we attempt to leave the premises."

"I'll meet you both at the side of the house. Give me five minutes." River spoke as he walked toward the window, shouldered it open and threw himself out of it with a loud flap of his wings.

Sissily and I rushed to see what he was up to and were relieved when we saw him coasting over the parking area where the pack kept the majority of their vehicles.

"You sure he will be, okay?" I asked Sissily as I looked at Jack over my shoulder, my fingernails digging into the wood of the windowsill. Logically I knew that we had to go and put an end to the insanity overtaking my life, but I also worried about the kid. I'd never admit it, not even to save my life, but Jack grew on me.

I liked the little pest a lot more than I should have.

"Yes." Reaching for me she squeezed my forearm reassuringly and my entire body visibly relaxed. "The flames will disappear as soon as anyone with the same DNA as Jack comes near them."

"Thank you." The cough that covered my mumble spoke volumes about my emotional state.

Hecate help me! I was turning into a pathetic emotional wreck.

Chapter Six

After we waited for River to hotwire a car and pick us up under the window of my room, I had to dangle Sissily above the open truck a good ten minutes while she kept hissing threats on my life if I dropped her, only to end up stuck with both of them in the middle of nowhere in a tin can with dozens of Mazzikin chasing us.

There were times when I asked myself why I couldn't just stay locked up in a room where shifters fed me, took care of me like I was an infant and I didn't have to do anything apart from rake up Danika's credit card balance with online shopping. Who knew that La Perla had an overnight delivery for a pushup bra in dusky pink directly from Bologna, Italy? Not me until a week ago, that's for sure. That damn book must've crossed some wires in my brain because there I was, bouncing in the back seat of a pickup truck whose tires found every pothole and rock on the dark dirt road we took to escape pack lands.

As we suspected the spirits gave chase, forgetting all about tormenting the shifters. Why would the cursed spirits care about wolves when they had me where they want me? The problem was not that all of them followed us as if I was the Piper and they were the rats. It was the fact that the shrieking increased in pitch and in volume. I was developing a killer migraine which by default made me very murder-y. Pretty soon we might get the attention of the humans, too.

If that happened, I would just jump out of the moving vehicle and hope to break a neck or something. That would be a better alternative than explaining any of it to my grandmother. I haven't seen Danika since our last fiasco with the kidnaping of Amber and Jack and I wanted to keep it that way.

"I'm assuming we just show up wherever you think this gate is and they'll be more than happy to let us in?" I nervously prattled but Sissily with her great hearing heard every word I said in the noisy truck while I twisted and turned to check on our pursuers through the back window. As freaked out as I was, I still wanted to double check that all of them followed, and none were left behind that could harm the pack. Tiny rocks peppered the underside of the truck making it sound like a machine gun was going off next to my ear.

Why don't they design a convertible pickup truck? That should totally be a thing if you ask me.

"Oh, definitely." She told me, widening her eyes as if she couldn't contain her excitement for sharing the information. "Especially for you, they'll have a cloud soft bath robe, slippers, and a flute of Champagne so that you are fully relaxed for the experience. It includes all of the a la carte places in Hell for Hazel Byrne."

"You're such a jerk." My tone was stern because I wanted to sound insulted, but my mouth was quirking at the corners.

"It's one of my many talents as you know." She smiled tightly at me over her shoulder before darting her gaze around and swallowing thickly at the sheer number of demons surrounding the truck.

"We will make it there." River had wanted to reassure us, probably aware of our state of mind from all the nervous energy assaulting his senses and filling up the closed confines of the truck but he had to raise his voice to be heard over the screams, which only sent a shot of adrenaline to spike up my heartbeat.

"I know we will, Blackman, no need for reassurances. Just watch the road, please. I can fix the problem with the Mazzikin if it becomes unbearable now that we are away from people we don't want to harm. I can't fix it if we end up wrapped up around a tree trunk."

His eyes locked on mine through the rearview mirror for a second and my heart skipped a beat for a totally separate reason than the immediate danger to our lives. The reminder of the bombshell followed with a painful stab through my sternum, and I glared at him. His look turned knowing, and a smirk graced his lips, which only darkened my mood if that was even possible.

"Or you can stop, and I'll be happy to sit back and watch what kind of an effect the Mazzikin have on pigeons such as yourself."

"Come on you two." Sissily barked twisting in the front seat so she could look down her nose at us like some warden. "Don't you dare start because I just about had it with you two. It's bad enough knowing at any moment I could turn into a mindless monster and all it'll take is a touch of a Mazzikin. If the alternative is listening to your bullshit, I'll just jump out of the moving truck right now."

I clamped my mouth shut and faced the window more

out of shame for acting immature than anything else. I think I heard River mutter an apology to my best friend, but I couldn't be sure. My heart was hammering in my chest and white noise was mixing with the shrieks of the Mazzikin in my ears. We were still on the dirt road rocking away like a sailboat in a middle of a hurricane; so that didn't help matters either.

Trees loomed in front of the pickup truck illuminated by the headlights, their branches ominously reaching for us, grabbing at our vehicle, and forcing me to grind my teeth from the scratching sounds joining the chaos around us. If anyone told me, I would be looking forward to going to Hell an hour prior I would've called them a liar. As things stood, I found it difficult to not yell at Blackman to speed up. I mean, he was driving as fast as he could all things considered.

My phone decided to voice its objection for being glued to my butt through the fabric of my jeans all day. At first, I couldn't recall why the sound sounded familiar until Sissily turned to me and looked pointedly at my ass.

"Oh!" With a depreciating curl of my lips I yanked it out and the glare of the screen made shadows dance around the otherwise dark cabin of the truck.

A group of about four spirits judging by the extorted heads slammed into the back door and the truck rocked harshly to the right. I almost dropped the phone. After a few expertly executed juggling tricks, I snatched it midair and rushed to answer it before whoever was calling hung up.

Needless to say, I should've let it go to voicemail.

"Hazel Byrne, what in Hecate's name do you think you are doing?" Danika's voice came through the speaker of my iPhone sharp as a whip. My spine snapped straight. "Mr.

Greywood just called telling me you are off pack lands and there is a horde of demons following the vehicle Mr. Blackman is driving."

"Are you worried about Blackman or me?" My drawl earned me an indignant huff. I couldn't care less.

"Tell Mr. Blackman to turn around and return you to the alpha." My grandmother hissed probably hoping to keep her voice down so no one would hear her reprimanding her insufferable granddaughter. My eyes rolled to the back of my head.

"I'm not a pair of pumps someone borrowed for a night out, Danika. River knows better than to do anything I don't want him to do." I hissed right back.

Sissily lifted her eyebrow at me not even trying to pretend that she's not listening to my conversation.

We hit a deep pothole on the road and the truck bounced up harshly knocking my head on the roof hard enough to rattle my teeth. Groaning from the pain, I tightened my grip on the driver's seat, my nails digging into the fabric in hopes to stay seated and not be a pile of limbs on the car floor. The Mazzikin, not wasting the opportunity, rushed us from all sides like a cloud of flickering ghosts, creating a terrifying picture of distorted faces coming at us full speed scary enough I had to swallow a scream. Cold sweat trickled down my back and I watched in horror as their incorporeal forms became tangible just as they connected with the vehicle rocking it hard enough, I could count the tiny rocks lined up like soldiers on the dirt road ready to ricochet and ping on the underside of the truck.

When we slammed back down to drive on all four wheels and not just two, I harshly bit my tongue and my mouth filled with the coppery taste of blood. Naturally, I blamed Blackman for it, so I slapped the back of the driver's seat in anger. River glared at me for a second before he had to focus on the road and the increasing number of trees crowding around our truck. You'd think it'd deter the spirits from chasing after us, but you'd be wrong. Unlike us, they allowed the towering oaks to pass through them. We were the only schmucks that had to dodge obstacles.

"Are you listening to me, Hazel? Are you hurt?" Danika shouted and lost all of her holier than thou attitude. Pure undiluted worry leaked through the speakers. "Turn that car around immediately Mr. Blackman and return my granddaughter to safety or you will answer to me."

The truck started slowing down.

"Don't you dare, River." I hissed at him leaning forward in case my tone was not convincing enough. Instead of his seat I latched onto his shoulder, digging my nails in as hard as I could. "Keep driving."

Blackman glanced really fast at Sissily who was already nodding like a bobblehead and stabbing her finger at the road ahead, silently agreeing with me that we need to continue. Smart woman didn't want to say a word and get on Danika's shit list, so she was running for first place in the competition of being the best meme. I was a different story. I was Numero Uno just by being born, and the rest of the list had to live up to my standards of a screw up to stay on it.

The truck jumped forward and increased its speed.

"Hazel, I know you are hoping that Leviathan will give you all the answers you seek but I assure you he doesn't have them." My grandmother tried a different tactic, softening her tone and all. "Stop being hotheaded. Can't you see you are exposing River and Sissily to danger in the pursuit of what? More questions and uncertainties? Don't you think

I've already tried most of the things you are coming up with?"

My mouth opened to tell her to get lost because I just about had it with her manipulations and lies but that's all I had time to do. The front of the truck hit something and we pitched forward the tail of the vehicle bouncing high and tossing us into a tailspin of swirling metal. Sissily screamed but I couldn't even look to check if she's okay. The door on my left was wrenched open and my own scream joined that one of my best friend. Fingers wrapped around my arm, and I was yanked out of the airborne truck so hard something cracked in my neck sending a sharp pain through my shoulders and skull. The phone slipped through my fingers and Danika's voice faded into the chaos of strong winds, screaming Mazzikin and fear clouding my mind. The last thing I saw before darkness took me in its embrace was Sissily's blonde ponytail flapping in the wind like a white flag of surrender and chocolate brown eyes staring intently into mine. As I was passing out white wings closed in around me.

Chapter Seven

I have woken up in all sorts of awkward situations in my not so long existence. Hecate knows I'm the furthest thing from a saint if you've ever seen one. I've done the walk of shame dressed in my clubbing clothing in the early hours of the mornings more times than I could count. Not a stranger to hangover headaches, I knew all sorts of remedies to cure it if I found myself in a pinch. So, when I peeled my eyelids open with too much effort, I immediately wished to die so I could escape the sharp pain stabbing my temples; it spoke volumes about the state I was in. The shrieking was still going strong and not helping the beating of war drums in my skull at all.

Lesson 14: *Pain is always good. It means you are still alive although most of the time you'd be wishing for it to be otherwise.*

My stomach dropped when my body wobbled strangely, which brought my attention out of my internal musings and to the present. Two things became clear at once. I was in the air and the only thing preventing my death was a strong arm wrapped around my lower back. The Mazzikin were still around although for whatever reason they stayed about a couple of feet away from me, still screaming from the top of their lungs.

From us, to be correct since I saw River's impressive profile the moment, I raised my head. I could tell he was straining to keep us moving but he still had a tight smirk on his face.

It was starting to irk me that my life was turning out to be a shit show where everyone was having fun but me.

"She's awake." The bane of my existence announced for no reason, shouting it to the night stretching before us not bothering to glance my way. Sissily poked her head out from his other side, and I could see the relief written all over her face when we locked eyes.

"Disappointed?" I asked River, then blinked at his profile because I was unsure if I said it out loud to him or just thought it. After a long second of no comment coming my way and without moving too much in case, he decided to drop me, I tried to see where we were pressing my mouth firmly shut in case the contents from the late dinner that we had what felt like a year ago came out. With each flap of River's wings, I was getting a horrible case of motion sickness. Seeing that my best friend was not hurt lifted a mountain that was pressing on my chest, and I was already lightheaded because of it without feeling like something was tugging me gradually towards the horizon.

Lights were blinking from below us. At least they looked like lights from whatever I could see from the spirits darting all around us like a swarm of bees, so at least we were out of that cursed forest. I felt better knowing that if I fell, I would splatter on the ground like a ripe melon instead of being impaled on a tree like a skewer. Perspective was the key to happiness. Another thing I learned was very important if I wanted to keep my sanity.

"Almost there." Blondie finally turned his head to look at me and my lower belly tightened from the intensity of his gaze. "Hold on." With no further warning his arm tightened around me and I swallowed a scream when we dipped low in the air increasing in speed as he shot like a bullet toward the ground while I was clinging to him like a spider monkey.

I'm sure everyone would agree that I would've had a lot to say about the situation, or even cause a scene, but the truth of the matter was, I was afraid. What could've been probably the first time in my life I was genuinely and utterly rendered speechless because I was scared. There are a number of ways I saw myself going down and most of them were epic if I could say so myself. None included Mazzikin possession. In general, I was a control freak. Being killed because I was a nutcase with no control of my actions was my worst nightmare.

First that damn book, now the demons.

A body of water came into view, which at first, I mistook as my mind playing tricks on me. The tears gathering at the corners of my eyes were turning everything distorted so it took me a long moment between that and digging my nails into River's arm to realize that it was indeed the reflection of the moon I was seeing in the distance. Nervously, I glanced around at the Mazzikin; although they seemed more agitated, they stayed away from our little bubble of safety.

Blackman swayed slightly and I dug my manicure harder into his arm, breaking skin. Worried he might decide to drop me if he was hurt and couldn't carry my weight any longer, I summoned all the courage I could to release him with one hand so I could point at what looked like a lake. As we got closer, I realized it was Lake Erie.

"Aim there, River." I shouted at him. "It'll cushion the fall." At the same time, he shot me a glare like it was my fault he skipped shoulder day at the gym and couldn't carry Sissily and I easily. My best friend was done dangling silently on the other side as well. I caught a sight of her arm flicking the air in front of her and ropes of fire burst from her fingertips smacking the demons who got closer while I was not paying any attention to them.

My heart skipped a beat.

Whatever was keeping us safe was wearing off and they were crowding us more and more with each inch of altitude we lost. Sissily was saying something too from the other side but between the screams and the flapping wings her voice was lost to my ears. Blackman, however, was nodding so I took that as a good sign. Especially when he twisted harshly and pointed us at the lake as we increased speed going down.

Fear clawed a hole in my gut for more reasons than just breathing my last breath. Ever since the spell backfired with the Mazzikin my magic turned its back on me. By now I should've lit up like fireworks but not a spark was to be seen. Fortunately, I had other, more crucial things to worry about than the lack of powers when I needed them most.

Suddenly the wings that loomed over us like an umbrella retracted when he tucked them closer to his body and we zipped faster than I thought possible going down. I'd never been the praying type, but I'd be lying if I said I wasn't praying to anyone that would listen to save our lives. Many things went through my head, dumb ones like maybe I should've kissed River at least once before I splattered like a water balloon in the middle of Cleveland, Ohio.

Instead, I snuggled closer to his body and closing my eyes I braced for impact. It didn't happen immediately, so naturally I cracked my eyelids open which I regretted instantly. A shriek louder than the Mazzikin ripped from my throat.

We were dropping deadweight aimed right at a glass building that was placed half on solid ground, the other half over the lake. The building itself was made entirely out of glass at first glace and resembled a pyramid. Under a closer inspection, it was made from different shapes you'd think a toddler stacked up learning forms in a jumbled mess that somehow stayed standing. I would've been impressed if my life was not flashing before my eyes. Ropes of flames were still twisting and turning over the water, cutting a path between the demons that gave us a clear view of the place where we were going to die, a courtesy of Sissily who unlike me through this whole ordeal was useful. So, as things were, all I could do was continue to scream.

Until the only sound echoing through the night was my embarrassing screech.

That too cut off abruptly when we were jerked to a stop as if an invisible hand plucked us from the sky. What was left was the drumming of my heartbeat between my ears which was making me nauseous and dizzy. And River's arm which tightened around me so painfully you'd think someone was trying to steal me from him.

"I can't breathe." My rasp sounded too loud to my ears forcing me to wince. At least the pressure loosened around my ribs, so I was able to suck in much needed air. Now that my lungs were not deprived, I could also notice a lot of things which were previously unimportant to my brain.

"They're not attacking." The ill attempt at pointing at the Mazzikin had my hand flopping around like a dead fish.

"Maybe we can go down, River?" Sissily's tone was raw and hoarse telling me I wasn't the only one screaming in the last hour. "I can think better when my feet are touching the ground."

"The goddess didn't have airborne activities in mind when she created me either." I was under no obligation to support my best friend at all times, but I did so anyway the very second Blackman turned his peepers my way. "I was made to cruise low where my toes can graze the mother."

Sissily groaned. "Save her from her misery, I beg of you, River. She'll keep talking the longer we stay up here."

"What's that supposed to mean?" My indignation was accompanied by a smug, low chuckle from Blackman that did dumb things to my neither region. Damn him and his stupid pigeon feathers.

"Anyone care to enlighten me, why the Mazzikin are not attacking. Two seconds ago, I had flash backs from my life and now they are looking at me like I am a curiosity to them." Uneasiness clawed at my insides as I watched the spirits floating around us, as if they were not trying to burst my ear drums a second ago.

"It is rather peculiar how they stopped shrieking the moment we entered the space above the lake." River gazed thoughtfully around us with a line forming between his brows, but his arm tightened around me, and I am guessing Sissily too.

"They do say curses do not carry over water. I don't suppose you know who can place a curse on spirits, do you Blackman? That should be right up your alley, only pigeons like yourself can screw with demons, correct?" If I sounded smug, it's because I was. Not like I was supposed to die anymore and the Mazzikin was staying away from us for now. In the meantime, I needed someone to blame, and Blackman was the perfect candidate.

"I am not sure that is the case here Hazel." Sissily leaned over Blackman so she could look at me. "I can't be sure, but I think we entered a protection circle when we entered the building. If I am not mistaken, we are at the right place.

"I will have to agree with Sissily, I have been trying to get us on the ground for the last few minutes with no luck". My head jerked to the side so I could gape at Blackman who so casually told us we were stuck two hundred feet in the air dangling like Christmas ornaments above Lake Erie. "We're staying here for now."

"I don't know how to break it to you Blackman, but if my boots don't touch the ground in the next five minutes, I will pluck you feather by feather till there is nothing left." Ignoring the glare Sissily was shooting my way, I narrowed my eyes at River to ensure that he knew I wasn't kidding.

Strong winds pelted us from all sides, swinging our bodies this way or that, despite the fact that I hated being stuck with River with no escape route in site, I tightened my hold on him, now that the screeches of the Mazzikin were gone, nothing prevented me from hearing his heart beat thumping across his rib cage to mine. That did all sorts of dumb things to my brain that I tried so hard to ignore.

What rubbed me wrong was not that I couldn't resist Blackman at all costs to save my life, it was the fact that he was aware of it if the smirk twitching the corner of his lips was anything to go by. The jerk knew what he was doing to me, and he loved every minute of it.

I fucking hated it!

"So, River do you come here often?" My drawl earned

me a raised eyebrow which I returned with as straight a face as I could.

"Before I dropped my phone, which I am assuming happened when River yanked me out of the truck, I am pretty sure Danika was about to tell me something regarding the demons and the reason the exorcism did not work on them." After an awkward silence stretched between us with my attempt at humor, I decided to put River out of his misery. The situation we were in was more important than making his life miserable. "Looking at them now, I get this sinking feeling, they were not sent to harm the pack or anyone else. I could be wrong, but I think we were herded like sheep, and they have us right where they want us."

"I believe you are correct Miss Byrne. The fact that we can't land, nor can we fly away from here confirms your suspicions." River muttered under his breath, intently staring at all the Mazzikin floating passively around us.

"Okay, I need both of you to shut up and help me come up with a solution that will place the soles of my feet on the ground." Sissily hissed at us through clinched teeth which she followed by blowing a piece of hair out of her face, harsh enough to plop it to the back of her skull.

"If I didn't know any better, I'd say you are afraid of heights girl." I poked at her. If looks could kill, I'm pretty sure I would've been dead by now. I had to back track before she decided to zap me with magic. "Take it easy there, killer, it was only a joke. I would rather be down there as well…"

My voice trailed off when gurgling sounded from the lake below us accompanied by large bubbles that rose to the surface of the lake toward us. River twisted around pulling both of us with him in his futile attempts to escape whatever was about to make an appearance. His wings stretched wide behind us forming a flimsy protection from what seemed to be a goddess forsaken kraken. Tentacles as wide as my waist wiggled up in the air reaching for us and although it couldn't get anywhere near, I still kicked at it.

Tingles shivered up my spine as my brain produced all types of worse case scenarios, and in none of them did I escape the creature that was eyeing us from below the lake. I bet it was coming up with ideas on how to best snatch us. Now I knew how a fly would feel when a frog catches sight of it.

"Sissily don't just sit there, zap it." Not daring to take my eyes off the octopus-thingy, I plastered myself to River, they will have to surgically remove me from him when we end up landing.

"The only thing I will do is piss him off, I think this a perfect situation to test your magic." My best friend pointed out very reasonably, which reminded me.

"About that. Do you remember that you were the one pushing the Mazzikin back this whole evening?" Not waiting for an answer, I smiled tightly at her. "I can't use my magic, it's gone."

"What do you mean it's gone?" Both of them shouted at the same time.

"Funny story, after the failed attempt at exorcism, it kinda fell dormant. All through the night I had a roller coaster ride of emotional trauma and nothing," Sticking my arm out, I wiggled it in their faces." See, not even a spark. Nothing."

"It could be because me and River are here." Sissily ever the helpful rushed to assure me that there was nothing wrong with me. "You know that your magic always pulls back around people you care about."

"Right." My snort echoed in the silent air around us." I

will never feel safe around River when it comes to my magic. Every time I see his face, all I can think about is how would a fried pigeon taste. All joking aside I think I screwed something up or that spell backfired. Can you imagine if I turn out to be a dud again? I would pay to see Danika's face then."

"It could be all the blood loss too." My best friend reached across River to give my arm an affectionate squeeze. "You have been bleeding left and right the last month or so every chance you get. Despite your Fae lineage, you are a witch after all. No blood, no magic I am afraid."

"You say such sweet things." I deadpanned although I did smile tightly at her to soften the sting. She meant well and it was not her fault. My life was all screwed up, if anything, her friendship made it bearable.

"Get ready ladies," Blackman flapped his wings and shifted us sideways so that we could float away further from the creature below us. "Here it comes again."

All things considered, it was kind of nice of Blackman to let the banter between Sissily and I to go on as long as it did. Not like I would have admitted it to anyone, but despite all of his faults, he was a decent guy. As a friend, nothing else. He would have been a perfect candidate to serve as a joy ride, but I changed my ways. Okay fine, I just don't want to kill anyone, and I light up like a Christmas tree. A geyser shot from the lake high enough to spray us from head to toe. River tried to shield us with his wings but was not fast enough. Brown stinky water dripped down my face, sending rage spiking through my veins.

Horrified, I looked down and my five-hundred-dollar blouse and wanted to cry. Yet another designer piece ruined by cursed demons with the rate they were going, I had every intention to ask Leviathan for reimbursement when I ended up finding him, of course.

"Incoming!" Sissily warned, flinging her forearm in front of her face.

Following her example, I did the same, but I should not have bothered. River tucked both of us closer to his body and cocooned us in the circle of his wings so he could take the brunt of the impact. We knew we were stuck up in the air, so he took the risk to protect us rather than to keep us afloat. I should have known something horrible was about to happen. I didn't expect it.

Something solid slammed into us from the side so hard that I lost my grip on River. The sound of a bone cracking was like a bullet firing next to my ear. To hear Blackman shouting in pain was something that I did not think I would hear. Despite the fact that I was plummeting toward the churning lake, my heart hurt from the sound. Sissily's scream told me that she was yanked away from us too, and although I twisted and turned to see them too, the only thing in front of my eyes was the foaming dark waters from the lake.

There was no time to scream, pray, or even laugh at the absurdity of it all.

I was so close to it I could smell the fishy stench of the tentacle waiting at the bottom of the lake. Anger stabbed me at the center of the chest that whoever it was gunning for my head had no decency to look me in the eye before they took my life. I didn't care about that either. What I did care about was that fucker was about to kill my best friend and the guy that has been the thorn in my side for so long.

A slimy tentacle triumphantly curled around my body and tightened hard enough to make my bones grind. It only fueled my rage more. It yanked me under water for a second after I filled my lungs with air.

And that is when it happened.

That was when my magic had had enough, my skin burst into shimmering words of forgotten tongues and the lake exploded from rays of light as if the sun took a dive in the middle of Lake Erie and illuminated everything within sight.

Take that Kraken.

Chapter Eight

A slow clapping brought me back from the pit of nothingness that I was enjoying more than I should. With a groan, I burrowed my face into the soft pillow hoping whoever it was thinking they were a comedian and applauding my ability to sleep would simply go away. It's been a while since I felt as good as I did at that very moment. The best thing was that I don't remember bleeding at all before the night was over and sleep took me.

I would take that as a win any day.

"That was quite impressive Miss Byrne, no wonder your grandmother has been keeping you under the radar for so long." A low seductive chuckle sent shivers under my skin and my eyes popped open.

Shooting out of bed like an arrow, I landed in a crouch next to it with arms raised ready to punch whoever thought it was their place to be inside my bedroom uninvited. That only amused my intruder more. He full on laughed in my face.

I blinked.

I then blinked some more, because wherever I was, it was sure the hell not my bedroom. If the gothic décor was not any indication, the surfer dude with his board shorts and his impressive six pack was a dead giveaway. When I said dead, it was pun intended.

"Who in Hecate's name are you?" Taken aback, I dropped my arms and took a few steps away from him. Whoever, or whatever it was, it was not human, or alive for that matter.

"Charon at your services." The surf dude plopped out his arm with flourish as if we were attending a ball in eighteenth century England.

When he lifted his head and smiled at me with two rows of shark-like teeth that split his face wider than was normal, I regret opening my mouth at all and not playing possum when I woke up. Locks of blonde hair flopped over his forehead covering a bright red eye which spiked my adrenaline because the other eye had nothing, and a silver coin was sewn inside the socket. Reality socked me in the head so hard I staggered backwards when I recognized that cursed coin. Pained groans bounced off of the walls as I flopped back in the bed not caring that a demon could eat me alive if he so pleased. Because that's what he was, a resident of Hell.

"I am dead, aren't I? It finally happened."

Throwing a forearm over my eyes, I couldn't even look at the guy. Another thought hit me so unexpectedly, I jerked up in the bed and rushed to ask in a panic, "You haven't taken me across the river yet, have you. Danika can't yank me back if she feels like it, right?

"Oh, no, no, no my dear, you are not dead." Charon inched closer and goosebumps covered my skin. There was a chill surrounding his body that I can feel to the bone marrow, although physically I couldn't feel the cold on my skin at all. It was that terrifying feeling as if I crossed over an open grave and Death was breathing down my neck. "Who in the world would want you dead? Where would the fun be in that? The Fates finally played their hand. This is almost history in the making. I've been waiting for this… well let's just say a very long time for an immortal."

At the mention of the Fates my heart skipped a beat. He couldn't possibly know anything about the book, could he? As his smile stretched wider, my uneasiness kept growing. On its heels followed a worry that I was too afraid to voice, but I had no other option. I needed to know. Fingers curling into the covers, tangling, and twisting to a point it cut off the circulation of blood to my hands I summoned the courage to face the ferryman head on.

"Is Sissily alive? How about River? If they are dead, will you let me see their bodies, please? I will do anything you want." Everything came out in a rush, and I forgot I needed oxygen to function.

There. I could be polite if I needed to. A lump formed the size of a fist in my throat while I waited for his answer. The thing that the ferryman didn't know was that I was ready to claw the pits of Hell if I had to so I can get to Sissily. River was lucky that when I was freaking out, I forgot to pretend I cared nothing at all for him.

"As tempting as that may be -and believe me I would love to hold that over Danika Byrnes's head- it is against my nature to tell you lies." The light in his red eye increased, the iris flicking left and right across my face as if to search for something or maybe even read my thoughts. Can demons do that? I would have to ask Sissily when I found her. Please goddess make sure she's alive. "Your companions are alive although not yet awake." The creature informed me, all smiles and as polite as ever. "I will take you to go see them the moment they open their eyes. Until then you and I can have a little chat."

My mouth opened to tell him where to shove it with his little chat when the alarm bells started screaming in my head. There was absolutely no reason for me to be suddenly alarmed apart from some inner feeling that I should pick my next words wisely. My very life could depend on it. Alex and his advice, what felt like years ago, came to mind that an informed predator was a smart predator, and I took notice. So, in the same fashion, I opened my mouth, I clamped it shut and eyed him thoughtfully.

"Anything specific in mind that you would like to chat about?" Casually leaning on my elbow, I flicked invisible lint off the covers pretending it was no concern of mine what he wanted to waste time on.

"There it is." Charon crooned and grinned at me proudly like I was a monkey performing some amazing trick. "The infamous Byrne cunning. I have missed it so very much." Clapping his hands excitedly he was practically vibrating on the spot.

"How many of us have you met?" Dropping all pretenses, I decided to be honest and open with the ferryman. At that point what did I have to lose? Dread pooled at the pit of my stomach the longer he stared back at me without saying a word.

The question gathered on the tip of my tongue but the very thought of saying it out loud sent my heart punching to the roof of my mouth before dropping and splattering at my feet. I could tell he knew what I wanted to ask; he was eager to hear it as if he was waiting his entire existence for this very moment. The coward that I am, I looked down at my feet. That is when I noticed my magic shimmering under my skin, flickering and blinking as if to remind me that I was not alone.

"Did you meet her?" Swallowing thickly, I had to blink fast to stop the tears gathering around my lashes from trickling down my face. I did not have to tell him who I was asking about. The knowing glint in his one red eye, was blinding in its intensity. But I opened Pandora's Box, so here goes nothing. "Did you guide my mother across the River of Souls on the night I was born?"

"No one crosses the river without me knowing, if she has paid the price, I have granted passage. A curious little thing, aren't you?" Hunching down, so he could better look me in the eye, he cocked his head to the side and stood there like that for a minute. "So young. So naïve. To have all the wisdom within reach of your little hand, but no knowledge on what to ask to acquire it. How pathetic."

"Let's get one thing straight." Leaning forward, so he knows how serious I am by my body language and not just my tone, I glowered at him. "If you wanted me dead, we would not be wasting time chit chatting right now. That means you need something from me. Probably something that I will not willingly give you. Until you forcefully take what you want, we are going to play this game my way."

He appeared more excited with each word I spoke, which should've told me I lost before we even started. My name would not be Hazel Byrne if I did not see things through, and I'm nothing if not determined.

"Don't patronize me, you fucker. I almost took down an entire city in the human world thanks to the pent-up rage from years of bullying. Push me hard enough and I will blow a hole in here big enough that the archangels will come over for a cup of tea. Are we clear?"

"Crystal." Stepping away from me he moved all the way

to the wall and casually leaned on it like he was not trying to scare the life out of me two seconds ago. "Now, are you going to ask me the correct questions, or should we waste more time on useless blabber?" As if bored, he looked down at his nails, but a moment later he peeked at me through his lashes. "I had great expectations from you, Miss Byrne. Please do not disappoint me."

"Did you transport my mother…" The question trailed off when Charon's face fell like I kicked his puppy. My mind raced trying to recall every word he said from the moment I opened my eyes. He said it is not in his nature to lie to me, which means everything I ask, he will tell me the truth to the best of his knowledge. I just had to line up the words in the correct order.

Not well versed in the rules and laws of the demonic realm, I had no clue if he could tell me something unless I specifically asked him for the information. And who's to say he will be accurate with the answer unless I could also read between the lines or know roughly what the truth may be. Everything was so confusing I was developing a headache behind my eyeballs that was stabbing at my brain.

"Where did you see my mother last?" I figured if he could tell me in which part of Hell, he dropped her off, I could maybe find her later. After I made sure Sissily and River were okay, of course.

The idea spread equal amounts of trepidation and exhilaration through me. Did I want to see my mother? Probably. I've never really thought about it but now that it was a possibility, I thought I did. I had too many questions for her and none all at the same time.

"At the River of Souls." Charon spoke slowly and deliberately as if he was talking to a mentally unstable person.

"Oh geez, that was so much help, buddy. Thanks." With

a sigh I rubbed a hand over my face in hopes of removing the fog that was clouding my mind. My thoughts were racing, jumbling together until it was either do something to stop thinking or start screaming like the Mazzikin until they drove us to where they needed us to be.

"Actually, you know what? How about you take me to see Sissily and River now, m-kay? They don't mind when I wake them up. I don't care where or if you've seen my mother or not."

Something akin to disappointment passed across his features but I was beyond the point of caring about trying to impress him. I needed to find my companions and get the hell out of dodge before Charon decided we might be a good distraction to his boredom and kept us as pets.

"You do not fear me, Miss Byrne." Pushing off of the wall he was leaning on, Charon moved across the room to the tall dresser on the opposite side. Reaching for a trinket box, he slightly lifted the crystal lid the color of blood, but paused so he could turn and look at me over his shoulder. "It's quite refreshing, I must admit." My cocked eyebrow made him smile at me sadly. "Ah, right on time."

"Huh?" Confused I frowned at him not sure which one of us was the mentally unstable one.

"Your companions are awake. I'll take you to them now." The demon picked out a stone from his trinket box and curled his fingers around it as if it was the most important thing in his life.

I was up and at the door before he was done talking.

Chapter Nine

"Do you stay here alone?" rubbernecking I followed him down a long dark hallway so close my toes kept bumping his heels. "Sorry, it's pretty dark here and I'm worried I'll lose you if I don't walk close enough." Awkwardly muttering my fifth apology in the last two minutes I curled my lips in a pathetic attempt of a smile when he glanced back at me.

"Yes, I am alone in this domicile." Slowing down he turned to face me, and I jumped back like he would try to bite me. Embarrassment heated my cheeks, which he noticed immediately. "Having a healthy apprehension of an opponent you know very little about is smart, Miss Byrne. Nothing to be ashamed of."

"Hey," deciding to change the subject, since I was not a big fan of sharing my fears with randos, I asked something that bothered me from the moment we arrived over Lake Erie. "Do you know why the Mazzikin were acting so wacky when we tried to exorcise them? According to my gra...I think someone mentioned they might be cursed." I finished lamely.

A sinking suspicion that the ferryman had an unhealthy obsession with my grandmother made me not want to bring her up if I absolutely didn't have to. I don't know what it was but every time he mentioned her priorly a spike of unease shot through my sternum warning me that something was off. The tight press of his lips displaying his displeasure confirmed my suspicions, but luckily for both of us he didn't press the matter.

"Many things are not as they used to be in this realm." After a long look he turned forward and continued down the hallway scratching absently at his abs. "It's not just those that reside outside of the Underworld being affected. We all feel it."

"Feel what?" the toe of my boot tapped his foot again and I mumbled a quick sorry hoping not to distract him too much. "A curse?" The skin on my arms pebbled from the thought. I shivered.

"It never ends well when the Fates get involved and try to offset the power." Charon sounded distant, his tone raspy and hollow. "I told Lucifer a century or two ago that this was going to happen. But did he listen, of course not. What would I know about demon politics."

The mention of the Fates sent a spear of dread straight to my chest. Deep down I knew he was talking about the book, the magic deep inside me perked up as soon as his voice got that eerie tone to it, but I ignored it. Let's just all pretend that the pink elephant in the room did not exist. I was okay with it. Charon was okay with it. Hell, even the moving tapestry on my left was okay with it.

Wait what?

"Do the tapestries often follow your guests around here or am I in for a special treat?" My nervous snicker bounced off the stone walls and unashamedly I latched on to Charon's arm when the said tapestry giggled back at me.

Throwing caution into the wind, I turned to examine the tapestry that seemed to follow us down the hallway. I regretted it the same second when multiple pairs of eyes locked on mine. The giggle continued to echo around us, and it irked me that the Ferryman laughed in my face.

"It would appear that they like you," a genuine smile graced his lips thankfully not showing the two rows of sharp teeth. "They are all just infant devils learning the ins and outs of the realm before they are allowed to roam out of the portals. They are harmless. For now."

"Duly noted." I sounded cool and collected, but my heart was drumming across my ribcage the longer we walked down the seemingly never-ending hallway. "Is it much further before we get to my friends? Not to sound ungrateful, but I have places to go and people to see. Can we just move this along?" Hoping to sound like less of a bitch and prove Sissily wrong, because I can totally be a likeable person, I slapped his shoulder good naturedly.

The slap exploded so loudly in the empty hallway; it made the stupid little devils in the tapestry shrink back. Charon froze, his foot lifted off the ground as he was trying to take a step and turned to face me painfully slowly. Until that very moment, I didn't notice that I was still clutching his forearm with my other hand. Swallowing thickly, I followed his gaze and looked down to where my fingers were digging into his skin. Flickers of magic blinked in and out under my skin and trickled from my fingertips into the ferryman. Where my magic connected with his body his skin shimmered as if an illusion was being broken.

What my mortal eyes could see was the surfer dude with his perfectly formed six pack. What my magic showed me was a skeletal figure with gray leathery skin and black talons for finger nails as long as my arm. Gulping oxygen so I don't hyperventilate, I released my hold on him one finger at a time.

"Nice visual effects you got. We have the same in our coven to keep the humans away." Now that I have no physical contact with him apparently, I got more stupid. Instead of walking away like a normal person would, I elbowed him in the ribs and belted out a laugh to be the envy of a five-hundred-pound man.

Charon staggered back, his one eye widening, and I couldn't help the gasp that passed my lips.

"I have been told that they dropped me on my head many times when I was a baby." With a nervous chuckle I glanced left and right looking for an escape route in case he pounced. "It does damage to the brain I've been told."

"We are almost there." He mumbled after a long moment and whirled on his heel so fast I had to rush to catch up with him, so I didn't lose him in the darkness of the hallway.

Miraculously, I managed to keep my mouth shut until we reached an unassuming door to our left. When I thought about it, there were no other doors the entire time that we were walking the long hallway. It made me wonder if it was a ploy that the Ferryman did to keep me on my toes, and he could summon doors at any time he wanted and at any place in his home. This had to be it, right? It had to be his home. He was more at ease here than I was in Danika's house. All my musings came to a halt when he opened the door and I saw Sissily standing in the middle of the room with her hands on her hips and a scowl firmly on her face.

"Whatever she told you. I assure you it is not as bad as it sounds." My best friend stabbed her forefinger in the Ferryman's face. "She has a condition, and we forgot her medication back at the house. She's more docile otherwise."

"Seriously? I've been dying to find you just so you can throw me under the bus?" my glare earned me an owlish blink from her. "I swear I should've found a way out and left you to rely on Blackman to get your ass out. I'm sure you'd be stuck in an orgy in no time."

"Mr. Blackman is down the hall." Charon chirped helpfully but the glint in his one eye betrayed his amusement.

"I wasn't sure if you woke up swinging or disoriented not remembering your name." Sissily breathed under her nose as she rushed to exit the room and join me. "I figured we can play good cop, bad cop, just in case."

"In case of what? They give out awards for idiots in the Underworld?" staring daggers at her back I swaggered after them. "If that's the case I guarantee you, you'll have the gold medal."

"Don't be a jerk, Hazel." With a quick glance over her shoulder, she hurried to keep up with Charon who was stomping down the hall again. "I never know what to expect with you anymore."

I slowed down, hesitating. My gaze narrowed on Sissily's back; I braced myself for whatever was about to happen. "I'd been meaning to ask. Do you think Jack will be able to help Amber get out of the spell while we are gone?"

"No doubt." She waved a hand over her shoulder dismissing me as if it was nothing.

Grinding my teeth, I clenched my fists and jumped-kicked whoever that was in the lower back. With an inhumane screech, she went down on all fours, her ponytail flopping like a dead animal on the side of her head.

"Who are you and what did you do to Sissily?" I hissed

at the creature and kicked it in the chin when it twisted around to see me.

Head flying back, it flew a foot or two to the side, stopping when it smacked the wall. Instead of fighting back or attempting to run away, it threw its head back and started to laugh. Charon joined in as well, both of them guffawing, you'd think I just told them the funniest joke of the century.

"Where are my friends, demon?" it took great effort to speak through clenched teeth and my words sounded garbled. "Speak before Hell is left without a gatekeeper." Rage was churning inside me, and with hands shaking I allowed it to grow to a point where my skin felt too tight for my body.

"A little test, Miss Byrne." Charon waved me off, unconcerned. "No harm done, I'm sure."

Raising my hand, palm up, I released a stream of light at him, hitting the floor an inch from his feet. The stone exploded with such force we all went airborne and were flung against the walls, me included. Arms shaking, I scrambled back on my feet as fast as I could and rushed back to where I thought Charon landed. The second his blonde hair came into view I grabbed a hold of it and yanked as hard as I could.

It did nothing.

I couldn't move him at all apart from ending up with a fistful of hair. Since he made no sound, I doubt he felt it either. Panic that Sissily and River might be dead for real made me reckless; so, I started kicking at the pile of limbs with everything in me. At some point I heard myself yelling all sorts of obscenities too, but I was so gone I didn't understand a word of it. It felt like I was kicking, punching and screaming for hours when finally, a voice penetrated the anger fogging my head.

"Hazel?" I recognized that tone. I'd know it anywhere. "Hazel Byrne!"

Panting, with sweat dripping down my face I turned around to face the speaker. Through clumps of matted hair my eyes locked on blue ones as wide as saucers.

"Sissily?" unable to trust what I see I racked my brain to come up with something which will confirm it's really my best friend. As always, she saved me from my misery.

"Is that Charon? Oh, dear goddess, Hazel, please tell me you didn't kill the ferryman." With a groan she slapped a hand on her forehead. "No amount of scrubbing altars will get us out of this one with Danika."

"It is you." I breathed and rushed her, hitting her full speed like a train to wrap her in my arms.

"Oomph," she wheezed, all the air exploding out of her lungs when we connected. "Easy woman, I'm breakable. Who else would it be?"

"That." Not releasing her in case they tricked me and took her away, I pointed at the creature that looked like her. "It tried to trick me into thinking it's you."

"Pfft, as if that would work." Sissily hugged me back. "I don't have that big of a forehead."

"Neither the forehead nor the boobs actually now that I can see it better." Tilting my head, I finally took a good look at it.

"I thought you were glad to see me." she grumbled and pushed me away.

"I am."

"You don't see me insulting your mammary glands, now do you?"

"My mammary what?" I eyed her warily.

"The chesticles." She circled her hand in front of her boobs.

"Oh," snorting, I smacked the back of my hand on her shoulder while she sniggered. "Speaking of boobs. Let's go find River before we all end up paying child support to a demon."

Sissily laughed but I did not find it funny. The pigeon had no idea how to keep his zipper up.

Chapter Ten

"So, I have a question." We searched the long dark hallway for a good hour with nothing to show for it at that point. "How did you know that the lump I was kicking was Charon? He wasn't exactly recognizable."

"What? That was Charon?" she recoiled from me as if I had some contagious disease. "I was just saying that to stop you from killing whatever poor soul landed on the wrong side of your temper." With an outraged gasp she snatched my arm and yanked me to a stop. "You beat up Charon? You have got to be kidding me!"

"Ummm," pursing my lips I debated whether I should give an affirmative or play dumb. "Yes?"

"Are you asking me if you beat up Charon, or you are telling me you did?"

"Yes."

"Hazel!"

"Sissily."

Saying her name calmly, I removed her talons from my

arm. "I was trying to find you. Not just Charon. I would've kicked Lucifer's ass if he stood in my way."

She shot me a glare as I laughed, but really, I could not be mad at her. She was right, I did a stupid thing yet again that will cost us dearly later. Since River was still nowhere to be found I pushed that worry away for another day.

We walked on in silence, Sissily stewing in anger I had no doubt, until we reached a wooden door. There was no handle, no lock that I could see, nothing to suggest how to open it—except for my bestie trying to push it open with her shoulder but then realized it was too heavy for just us two to move. It didn't deter her, though. Grinding her teeth, she kept shoving until I had enough and decided to stop her. But not before I stood back a good ten minutes and laughed.

"Sissily, stop it." I grabbed her shoulders and pulled her away from the door when I was done chortling. "What are you doing? This isn't going to open like that."

Her cheeks were flushed with anger and frustration as she shoved me away. "We can't just stand here, Hazel! River is on the other side of this thing; I can feel it! We have to do something!"

I sighed.

She was right but there had to be a better way to open the door than slamming our bodies into an immovable object. Dislocating a shoulder did not help anyone. Thinking quickly, I scanned the walls in search of something that might help us; and my eyes landed on a small groove beside the door frame. Reaching out, I touched it gently before pushing my finger in further until I felt a slight bump and a soft click was heard. The door made a low creaking sound as it swung slowly inward allowing us entrance into what appeared to be an ancient temple-like structure filled with altars, statues, and a heavy scent of incense burning in urns across the room.

The area was dimly lit and filled with wavering shadows that seemed to stretch and reach out towards us like gnarled fingers. I shivered despite the warmth radiating from the lit candles, the walls, and Sissily's grip on my arm tightening as she stepped closer to me for protection. The short hairs on my neck stood at attention the deeper we ventured into the space.

"Hazel, do you... feel that?" she whispered, her voice trembling.

"No." I hissed at her, my eyes darting everywhere at once in case something jumped us. "The only thing I feel is your heel digging into my big toe." After a thick swallow, I couldn't help but add. "You need to lay off the Danish pastries, girl."

"If we were not in danger of dying, I swear to Hecate I was going to shove my heel where it doesn't belong, Hazel Byrne." She giggled nervously.

I chuckled slowly too, and together we scanned the area again for any sign of danger. My heart raced in anticipation as we moved deeper inside, expecting some kind of trap or a horde of demons waiting for us around every corner. Fortunately, nothing leapt out at us although I could feel countless eyes watching our every move as we ventured into the chamber until I felt his presence almost like a physical sensation on my skin. And I knew it was River. His presence was both familiar and foreign all at once. My gaze found him as if I knew he was there all along.

He stood in the middle of the room, his head bowed so low it was impossible to make out his features in the dancing shadows. His arms were tied behind his back and stretched painfully by metal chains preventing him from straightening up. He made no movement but still, something about him sent chills down my spine. Blackman seemed too still, almost lifeless; except for a faint glimmer radiating from his figure; like the aura shrouding him in secrecy and the power from his bloodline refused to abandon him even in Hell.

I knew this was not the River I had come to know – or even care about despite my better judgment - this was someone new… something else entirely and yet despite everything, he seemed strangely familiar to my heart. Even in his silence, I could feel a slight hint of sorrow coming off of him like a tangible force, which made me want to go over there and wrap my arms around him so I could shield him from the world.

An invisible force kept me rooted to where I stood—afraid that any sudden movement would break whatever spell held us both under its thrall in that moment. After what felt like hours passed in silence and I breathed through the onslaught of emotions clogging my chest, he raised his head ever so slightly as if my presence meant something to him, too.

River fixed his unblinking gaze on mine, holding me a prisoner, while time seemed to stand still for what felt like an eternity.

Sissily broke the silence with a single word: "Run!"

Sissily's warning to run shook me out of my trance and I followed her lead without hesitation. We were already in trouble and the last thing we needed was to get cornered by a horde of Adlet demons. I knew enough about them to know they were not something we could take on alone, no matter how skilled we are with a sword or magic.

But it was too late. Before we could even make it three steps, the room filled with an eerie whisper that grew louder as dozens of hideous looking demons resembling deranged orangutans rushed us from all sides. Troll-like bodies with fangs for teeth and pointed long ears along with long sloth-like arms made them seem like a perfectly shaped gargoyle that stood too long under the sun and kind of melted. Half elf-like and the other half distorted, they were more horrifying than facing a pack of werewolves. The air thickened with the scent of ozone as demon magic filled every nook and cranny and we staggered forward even though everything in me was telling me to heed Sissily's warning and run.

The whispering continued, loud yet barely audible, a haunting sound that made it harder for me to think straight as they inched closer. With all of my energy I tried to remember what I had learned about these creatures, but my mind felt like mush from the panic, the words stuck in my throat like glue when I tried to talk Sissily through our next move.

"Are those Adlet demons?" Sissily pressed her back to mine so we could defend an attack from all sides.

"Yeah, they look like an Adlet." Flicking my hand, I sent a stream of magic at the closest few, and with a hiss they flinched back a few steps. "I can't remember for the life of me what worked against them. Do you?"

"Ummm," she fried a couple that got too close to her before she answered. "I'm not one hundred percent sure but I think the way to get rid of them was something to do with vibration." Another string of fire burst from her fingertips before she turned her back to mine. "Just don't take my word for it. Remember what happened with the Mazzikin?"

"How can I ever forget. That was my idea too though I can't blame just you for it." I trembled from the memory of the screeching Mazzikin. "It's worth the try though. Be ready to go snatch River if it doesn't work."

"Got it." She followed it with a groan.

That's when it clicked. Adlet demons spoke using whispers instead of words which meant they were only able to influence humans who heard their call— supernaturals like us who can't be easily affected by verbal powers could defend against them with loud sound. Sissily was right, as always. Without wasting another second, I grabbed my best friend's arm and pulled her toward River while keeping an eye on the demons around us ready for anything else they might throw at us.

That's when Sissily stepped on my big toe again and I couldn't prevent the shout of pain that ripped out of me. My scream bounced off the walls and echoed in the vast chamber sending all the Adlet demons scattering like roaches when the light comes on. It hurt like a mother, and my foot was developing a separate heartbeat as it throbbed but at least we confirmed our theory.

We reached Blackman just before any demons did, which gave us enough time to blast his chains using our magic before bolting for the darkness outside where we were sure there would be no more Adlet demons waiting for us this time. If any strays stayed behind all I had to do was return the favor and stomp on Sissily's foot. She'll make any soprano opera singer proud if my recollection of previous incidents serves me right.

That girl can scream.

We stumbled out of the chamber with River in tow, both of us putting as much strength as we could muster into our escape. The hallway was eerily empty, and the air felt pregnant with tension, the only sound being our panting breaths and thudding feet. I couldn't shake the feeling that something or someone wanted us to go there and get River out. As if this was some game, they played, and we were the pawns they moved wherever they felt like on the board. Glancing at Sissily told me she found the situation suspicious as well.

We had to get out of this place as soon as possible and had no time to dwell on things, so I started running, dragging River and Sissily behind me, my heart beating wildly in my chest. Everything seemed to be going smoothly, which should've told us we were screwed, until we reached a dead-end down the cursed hallway of doom. There was no way forward but there was also no way back either; the door we came through had disappeared into thin air like it never existed in the first place, leaving the walls smooth and empty.

Even the tapestry abandoned us.

Panic surged through me as I desperately searched for an escape route; white noise thudding in my ears, but all I could find was more stone and the musty stench of wet, molded stone filled my nostrils and I gagged from it. Pulling the t-shirt up over my nose and mouth I turned to see Sissily doing the same with her tank top. We were stuck and had no clue what to do to get out of the place.

The disgusting odor amplified the longer we stood there and in a last-ditch effort to show my fury, I threw my arms forward and released all the pent-up frustration at the wall, screaming from the top of my lungs. Sissily and River slid down to the ground since I no longer supported Blackman's weight and he took my bestie down with him. Panic clawed at me that he was still unconscious, too.

My voice sounded like the cry of a wounded animal, bouncing off the stone walls and traveling deeper through the hallway in the direction we came from. It created an eerie, sad picture of what my life had come too. And I managed to take those I care about down with me too.

Disappointment had my blood boiling through my veins. I'd be damned if I went down this way. In my irritation, I slammed both my palms on the wall making it crack and tremble. Covering my head with both arms I ducked and rushed toward Sissily and River, sure that I had just buried us alive in Hell of all places.

How's that for a kick in the proverbial nuts?

Instead of dying slowly and fighting for a breath under a ton of rock and rubble, a door formed right across from where we were crouched in a pile of limbs with Sissily and I holding River between us. I wanted to cry with relief.

Sissily rushed ahead of me and pulled open a red door while I yanked Blackman up and practically draped him over me. Wobbling in my boots, I dragged him across the hallway. The entrance was leading us into an old dark room filled with cobwebs and dust, another reminder that we were definitely not in Cleveland, Ohio anymore. I never thought I'd miss the place but yet again I stand corrected.

The space stunk of decay, and I gave it a cursory glance in search of dead bodies which were thankfully absent. There were no demons waiting for us beyond this door at least, so I blew out a sigh, puffing my cheeks out like a chipmunk. We searched around trying to find another exit but came up short handed until my eyes widened upon spotting a small window set high up on one wall.

"Look!" I pointed at the path to freedom excitedly; and not waiting another second, made a dash for it.

It was either that or fully pass out from the horrible odors.

Chapter Eleven

"I should've known this would not be as easy as it looked." I threw over my shoulder at Sissily as we trotted down yet another musty passage. This one was narrow, with a low enough ceiling that I had to hunch my shoulders and duck my head to fit in it.

We carried River between us, me holding his legs and her gripping under his arms. You'd never guess the male was as heavy as an elephant. He looked so lean. Concern gnawed at my gut that he wasn't waking up, but I had to figure out a way out of here before I could start stressing about that. The important thing was that we had him with us. His aura gave me more apprehension too the longer I had skin contact with his body. There was something off about it, but I couldn't put my finger on it. As things stood, I would have to agonize about it later.

The air was getting thicker and harder to breathe with every step we took. I tried to keep up a steady pace, but it was getting increasingly difficult as River's weight threatened to drag me down. We had no idea how much further the exit remained or if we were going to find one at all. Hopefully there were no more traps or demons waiting for us, but I pushed that thought aside so it didn't make me panic and we kept going.

When we reached the end of the corridor I laughed and cried with sheer joy.

There right in front of me was a damn door. I've never seen anything more beautiful in my life.

"Girl, look." Twisting my body sideways, I glanced back at my friend. "This better lead to fresh air or I'm about to lose my shit."

"You're not kidding." Sissily huffed and pushed harder on River guiding me toward our salvation. "Don't just stand there staring at it. Move!"

We stepped through the heavy carved wooden door into a large circular chamber with a high domed ceiling and small circular windows that glowed softly from the blood red moon outside. A huge table dominated the center of the room and around it sat five hooded figures in deep meditation.

My heart began to beat faster when I noticed their eyes burning ice cold underneath their cowls – they all seemed to have sensed our presence and were now facing us, only their glowing irises were visible from deep within the hoods.

They looked ready to attack at any minute.

I motioned to Sissily towards the far side of the room where I spotted an ornate pedestal surrounded by small black candles flickering in a circle on the ground. Fluorescent green flames danced mockingly as we started inching closer to them. It was the only barrier we could place between us and whatever magic the creatures were going to pelt us with; so, I wanted to reach it yesterday.

We quickly increased our speed and dragged River away

from the sight of the demons and towards the mysterious looking column while they watched us silently - their eyes tracking us diligently, never leaving us for even a second as we moved closer and closer towards cover.

Standing right in front of the pedestal had my eyes widening when I saw what lay on top of it. Three red crystal keys were placed next to a vial of shimmering liquid, which had all the colors of the rainbow flickering through it. The air around them shimmered with an eerie green light warning me that it could melt my face off if I dared to touch the objects. This must be what they were guarding or praying to for all I cared, but one thing was certain, if I controlled the objects I could - probably would - control the demons. Or get us all killed.

One or the other.

"Whose idea was it to go find Leviathan?" I chuckled nervously under my breath and pointed my chin behind the pedestal to tell her to take cover. "That person should get fired!"

"I really want to punch you right now, Hazel." Sissily told me earnestly while panting but followed direction like a champ.

"If it makes you feel better, I really want to punch myself too." I meant every word of it. It couldn't be normal to get myself in these types of situations all the time, was it? I must be cursed or something just like the Mazzikin. At least they were safe now; and we were crouched behind the column while I was peaking sideways at the demons who have not moved yet.

Gathering all my courage though, I popped my head up, reached out my hand and made a grab for the vial and keys only to find myself frozen in place by some kind of invisible force field surrounding it. It felt like tiny needles were pricking my skin every time I attempted to touch the objects, making me gasp in pain. On the bright side, my face did not melt off. I'd take that as a win. Clenching my teeth and ignoring Sissily hissing at me to stop, I snatched the keys and tiny bottle.

The moment they were in my hand the world around us exploded.

Hands the size of my body stuck out of the stone walls, stretching above our heads toward the ceiling. Talon-like fingernails scraped at the stone floor and sides, making grooves that glazed over with a pale pink liquid that hissed and spat as it gurgled through them. The five robed figures lifted off their seats as one and glided around the table where they lined up shoulder to shoulder, standing taller than any man I'd ever seen; each of them had pallid skin as white as bone and eyes like burning ice that never left our hiding place for a second.

I felt my heart pounding in my chest as one of them stepped forward and raised its arms above its head with an eerie chanting noise that reverberated around us. The others joined and their deep voices curdled the blood in my veins. Sigils as red as blood burst into existence swirling around each hand of the demon, gaining in speed with each word out of their mouths. My feet started moving before my brain could think and soon, I was sprinting right at them, my magic gathering at the center of my chest.

There was a second where I worried, I might harm Sissily and River, but the nerve-wracking glares of the demons removed all of my doubts. I had to do something, or we all would die anyway. The chanting grew louder and more intense until it became so loud, I thought my head was about to burst like a grape from the pressure between my ears.

"Hazel, no!"

Sissily bellowed from behind the podium no doubt torn between following me and guarding River's unconscious form. I counted on my friend doing the right thing as always and not leaving anyone that was defenseless in the face of danger. That way if my insanity backfired, she would at least be safe. River, too.

Halfway to the five demons was all the time I had to reach when they decided to attack. The one with a burning sigil around each hand, the leader was my guess, lowered his arms and after tracking me for a few seconds, threw one of the spells my way. The sigil whistled in the air as it flew at me, spinning and swirling in an almost beautiful, mesmerizing way.

The thick scent of rotting flesh clogged my nose and whatever contents I had left in my stomach rushed to come out. Bile burned the back of my throat, but I summoned enough strength to warn Sissily to stay hidden.

"Stay there. I'll be fine." I ordered as coughing and gagging followed my brave declaration and I wiped my mouth with the back of my hand hoping that would make the disgusting taste go away.

I faced the demon leader, his eyes locked in a deadly battle for supremacy with mine. I hoped he could read the 'fuck you' I was sending his way too. He was determined to end me, and I was equally determined not to let him. Steeling myself, I focused on controlling my magic as it gathered in the center of my chest and ignored the stench that came from the hell spawn. With a roar, sparks exploded from both my hands and kept flying straight towards the demon leader who stood his ground with arms still raised above his head, glowing sigils spinning around them in a feral dance.

The other demons joined him now; two on each side forming a line ready to attack me in case their leader failed while other deep voices chanted spells from somewhere behind them like an invisible choir of backup singers. If the threat on my life was less, I would've laughed at the crazy images my mind was displaying about the situation. With that, my heart raced faster as each second passed but somehow a calmness drowned out all my fear and doubts that were trying to take me down. I didn't know what the future held but this much was clear - if these monsters won, everything I have gone through so far would have been for nothing.

My magic collided with the demon's sigil causing an explosion so strong that it knocked us both several feet in the air and away from each other - me landing on top of some sharp rock while the demon slammed into one of his buddies sending them both crashing into the table behind them and leaving an ugly dent the size of a giant fist in it. The chanting stopped abruptly as the other three stared at me in shock - it seemed no one expected me to pack a good punch and if I was being honest neither did I. Which was why I gaped at them like an idiot through clumps of my hair. A quick glance confirmed Sissily and River were alive and safe behind the platform, so with great effort I attempted to stand up and keep fighting.

"That's enough." A booming shout cut through the air like a blade, the words reverberating off the damp walls of the chamber. The voice that had haunted my nightmares echoed across the chamber, cutting through the silence like a storm. It was familiar, yet distant, and its power chilled me to the bone. Those two words sent shivers down my spine. All heads snapped to attention as the figure stepped out of the shadows like it was his right to own them. "What is the meaning of this?" the figure demanded.

I heard Sissily gasp in horror but thankfully she stayed hidden from view. The demon didn't need an introduction for me to know who he was. The vertical pupil and the sharp cheekbones which could cut glass announced him loud and clear. As Danika would like to say. Speak of the devil, and he would appear.

"Leviathan." I drawled and pushed off the floor so I could face him standing and not prostrate at his feet; although he enjoyed me being there by the look of his smirk. Not that it would help me much if I was on my feet. The top of my head would barely reach his pectorals. "Fancy seeing you here."

"A Byrne witch in my domain. One that can recognize who I am at that." He stepped down the two stone stairs and moved toward me while folding his hands at the small of his back. "What a pleasant surprise."

There was something in his tone. I couldn't really tell what tipped me off, but it was as clear as day. All of it. Charon, the little devil, chained River, and our crazy adventures through cheesy decorated chambers and creepy hallways...all of it was staged and it was all for his amusement. The gloating sparkling in his irises was not concealed as it should've been.

"Entertained yet?" dusting off my pants I glared at him. "Just to be clear I don't find any of this amusing at all. As a matter of fact, it kind of rubs me wrong."

"Is that so?" he murmured and circled me like a vulture would circle roadkill.

Silky black hair cascaded over his wide shoulders to the middle of his back like a waterfall.

All shiny and smooth it made my fingers twitch in need

to touch it and see if it's as soft as it looked. Long thick lashes were at half-mast hiding most of his impressive eyes that resembled a cobra attempting to mesmerize a prey before it devours it whole. Full, bow-shaped lips stood out stark against his angular face softening his features from intimidating to sensual and alluring.

"It is." My terse reply had him grinning at me and that was his biggest mistake when it came to me.

Pretty boys piss me right off by default.

"What are you going to do about it, little girl?" He stopped in front of me and leaned forward whispering the question seductively over my mouth, his long hair sliding over his shoulder to tickle the side of my face.

So, I kneed him in the family jewels as hard as I could.

Chapter Twelve

Leviathan doubled over; leaving no room for doubt that demon and human alike, a male is a male, and he would bow deeply when you crack his pecker. Whatever demons were left in the chamber scattered away so fast, I almost thought I imagined them being there when he roared in pain and clutched at his groin.

I must admit it was satisfying seeing him on his knees in front of me.

"Hazel, run!" Sissily gave up hiding and jumped out from behind the pedestal waving both arms frantically at me. "Don't just stand there." She growled furiously. "I said run damn you."

My bestie was already yanking on River, sliding his body across the stone floor one painful inch at the time. She was red in the face from putting her back into it, baring her teeth at the skies with each pull.

Shifting into a defensive stance, heart pounding in my chest, I prepared for the attack I hoped was coming. If it didn't come, I would've done something to keep the attention on me and away from Sissily and River. When all this started, I was expecting to have a chat with the archdemon. Thanks to my dumb temper I'd be happy if we walked out of here alive.

Maybe they should put me down like a feral dog.

Leviathan was changing and the shimmering air around him was contouring his kneeling form until it exploded into a towering black dragon with a spiked tail and a head the size of the pickup truck, we used to lure the Mazzikin away from the pack.

My heart skipped a beat but there was nowhere to run for me. His tail sliced through the air, narrowly missing me as I dived for the floor and rolled a few feet. It was a lucky save on my part because I dodged it at the last minute. I had to use my agility and speed to avoid his next strikes, finding openings to land quick blows wherever I could.

Adrenaline surged through me.

Each time I landed a hit, he roared in fury, his dark energy crackling around him and forcing me to take a step back to reassess. It was a dance of death we were doing, and I knew I couldn't afford to make a single mistake. Sissily, always by my side, used her own powers to support me, manipulating the air and fire to create distractions and keep Leviathan off balance.

The woman was something else. If witches had guardian angels, I had no doubt the goddess sent her in my life as one. But even with our combined efforts, the demon's power was overwhelming. He launched a devastating attack I didn't foresee, and I barely managed to conjure a protective barrier in time. The force of the impact sent me sprawling to the ground, pain shooting through my side as I slid over the stone.

"There is nowhere to run." Fuming in anger and fisting

my hands I glowered at the archdemon aka dragon at that moment and pushed myself up. "Isn't that right Leviathan?" the dragon roared at my accusations.

"You have finally lost your mind." Sissily snapped at me after the thundering roar, not giving up on her efforts to assist me. "I didn't fight to live through all the crazy just to be killed in some shithole in the middle of Hell because you act like a two-year-old. Fuck my life!" throwing both hands in the air she turned her anger on me. "Apologize to him at once."

Sissily's words had an immediate effect, and I felt a wave of shame wash over me. Even Leviathan was taken by surprise, the dragon's head swinging her way to better face her. I had let my anger get the better of me and endangered all of us in doing so. If anything happened to them, it would be my fault, no one else's. Taking a deep breath, I dropped my fists down and stepped forward to lower my head at Leviathan in a gesture of apology.

"I'm sorry," I said, my voice respectful and clear so he could hear me from ten stories up. His dragon was huge. "I should not have provoked you. It was foolish of me. Please, don't harm my companions, if you want revenge, you can take it out on me."

Leviathan eyed me through a narrowed gaze for a long time no doubt judging how sincere my apology was. I wasn't sure either about how sorry I was, but I was honest that I didn't want him taking it out on Sissily or River. After a while, the dragon grunted and the air around him shimmered again as he returned to his human form. His gaze met mine for a few seconds before his lips twitched slightly and he stepped forward. "You have guts kid," he said quietly, an odd hint of respect in his voice that I didn't expect from him. "But don't think your apology changes anything. Now, you owe me debt."

His arrogance made me angry again, so I clenched my hands into fists, and I glared at him defiantly. Apparently, he found my temper funny or maybe I played right into his hands because he fully smiled and watched me with renewed interest.

"We started out on the wrong foot, as humans would like to say." He told me conversationally, thankfully ignoring Sissily and River like they were not there. "Don't you agree?"

A ton of accusations and a few choice words were sitting on the tip of my tongue, but I swallowed them down and smiled tightly at him. Reminding myself that I had nothing to prove to the demon, it caused me for the first time in my life to stay silent. Who cares what Leviathan or any of them think anyway? I should worry about finding out information and getting Sissily and River out of there.

Then it hit me.

I narrowed my eyes on the too nice archdemon, who suddenly went from trying to bite my head off was having a polite conversation with me. He blinked those thick curly eyelashes at me a little too innocently for my liking. Something was off but I had no clue what. My magic pulsed inside me in agreement.

"Maybe we can just say we are all sorry and we can go home." Sissily muttered from the side while Leviathan and I were having a staring match.

He totally ignored her like she hadn't spoken.

My heart skipped a beat.

"What do you think about that Leviathan?" testing my suspicions, I watched him closely.

"If I am not mistaken it, was you that came to my domain, no?" one perfectly shaped eyebrow arrowed up.

He answered me but not Sissily.

"You have something personal against Miss Stormblood that you decide to ignore her, or…?" mimicking his expression I folded my arms across my chest. A sharp pain shot across my upper back, probably from the few falls I had, had in the last few hours but I managed not to wince.

"I can feel that you are not telling me something and I have a feeling I'm going to be pissed when I find out what it is."

Leviathan grinned.

My stomach dropped with dread.

Instead of arguing with the cursed demon I took a deep breath and stretched out my senses wondering if maybe another attack was brewing while he had our attention. I wouldn't put it past him to have us tricked and killed while I dumbly fell for his friendly chat. If the Ferryman taught me anything, it was to never believe anything I hear or see in the Underworld.

At first, I didn't notice anything strange. The thick scent of decay was still announcing the demonic magic loud and clear, even to those who can't sense it otherwise. The wet moldy stone mixed with it with its misty odor, and the eerie feeling of spirits and nightmares being present muddled my brain. Leviathan had his own powerful, seductive aura around him, tugging at my own magic as if trying his best to have my full attention.

Needy much?

Archdemons or any type of power figure in the supernatural world had their own neediness when it came to being the center of attention. Maybe my own attitude reflected that since I was around Danika my entire life. But even knowing that was not enough to convince me that everything was as it seemed. Urgency that I was missing something was drilling a hole in my stomach.

"I know something is off and I can tell you already that I'm going to be very angry when I find out what." Forking my fingers through my hair so I could untangle the knots, I avoided looking at him in hopes of catching what was going on through my senses. "And I usually do dumb things acting rashly and such when I'm angry. That gets Danika involved and it turns into a clusterfuck as you can imagine."

"You Byrne witches do have your way about you." Leviathan agreed readily, a knowing, almost pitiful look on his face.

"Wanna share what I'm missing then?" not beating around the bush I fully faced him. "I can tell something is up."

"You were inquiring about the Mazzikin when you first woke up in my realm, were you not?" He placed his hands at the small of his back in a creepily similar fashion like Charon at one point when he was guiding me through the hallway. Goosebumps pebbled my skin.

"Yeah, I wanted to know if they were cursed." A thought occurred to me, and I squinted at him. "Did you curse them so they could trick me into coming here? If that's the case, it was a waste of time and effort. I had every intention of finding you without it. All you did was make enemies out of Greywood's pack. A very bad decision if you ask me. Alex is not someone you want against you."

"Alex Greywood is not my concern." He brushed me off, pacing leisurely back and forward in front of me, his dress shoes clicking a steady rhythm on the stone. It was almost hypnotic. "He has a problem within his own family to fix and will now worry how easy it was for me to pay them to betray him."

Say what now?" Anger on behalf of my friend lit my blood on fire. "You paid someone from his pack to betray him? How? Who?"

"So temperamental." Leviathan chuckled glancing at me from the side of his eye. "Which is it, little girl? You want to know what you are missing here or who betrayed your dear alpha?" Pausing in his pacing he made sure I saw the triumph written all over his handsome face. "You can't have both, I'm afraid."

"Hazel?" Sissily sounded freaked out and my head snapped in her direction. She was crouching next to the still unconscious River, a look of horror twisting her features. "Ummm, I think something is seriously wrong with River."

My chest tightened, when Leviathan snickered at the panic in her tone, I rushed to where she was placing Blackman's head in her lap. When I saw the grayish color of his skin and the bluish tint of his lips my heart stopped beating. Head jerking up I looked at the archdemon who was looming over us while gloating at his cleverness.

"What's wrong with River?" Pushing the words through clenched teeth, I glared daggers at him. All the blood drained from my head as I watched the smile on Leviathan's face grow.

"What's wrong with him?" I screamed at the prick.

"Hazel, please." Sissily latched onto my forearm holding me back when I attempted to jump on the archdemon and beat the answer out of him. "We need to know how to save River. Please don't make thing worse."

"You should heed the warning of your friend." Leviathan told me conversationally, and I really wanted to punch him then. "But all things considered it's not as bad as it looks."

"What is not as bad? River dying or me skinning you alive?" My comment made the demon throw his head back and laugh while my best friend dug her nails into my skin until she made me bleed. "Sorry. What do you want so you can tell me how to help my friend?" for Sissily's sake, and River's, I swallowed everything I wanted to say out loud.

"He is not dying." Leviathan seemed almost insulted I would dare to suggest he was a murderer. "His angel blood does not agree with his choice of visiting my realm." Inching closer he peeked at the unconscious River as if he were a bug under his shoe. "He knew what could happen to him if he ever stepped foot here, yet he still came willingly."

Sissily and I looked at each other then blinked up at him in confusion. Say what now?

"Why in Lucifer's name am I wasting time with this?" Apparently not understanding his diabolical tactics made the archdemon cranky. He tossed his hands in the air in frustration. "He is changing." He told me slowly like I was dumb or something. "The longer he stays here the closer he is to becoming a fallen."

"Oh, River." Sissily gasped, covering her mouth with her hand.

Chapter Thirteen

I don't know what was worse. Knowing that my fucked-up life was going to cost River everything or that he stupidly rushed to help me knowing it could happen. I wanted to be angry at him.

I really did.

Staring at his handsome face with his eyes closed and his lips slightly parted made my chest hurt, however, and I couldn't find it in me to be angry with him. All I could do was suck in air through a straw since no amount of inhaling could inflate my lungs as it should. I wanted to cry. Hell, I wanted to scream to the heavens about how screwed up the situation was. The moment I felt his aura and it felt familiar, yet not, I should've known something was wrong.

As always, instead of paying attention, I selfishly cared only about what I wanted. What I need. Who cared about the rest of them? Obviously, it was not me.

Before I could embarrass myself further by bawling my eyes out, River slowly opened his lids and looked straight at me. Sucking in a sharp breath I froze, held suspended by the intensity in his irises. His gaze bore into mine and for a second the world around me stopped as if only us two were left standing there, connected by an invisible bond that bound our hearts together. I felt it thrumming like a string between us filling me with warmth. It was like looking into an abyss where all the feelings submerged within me surfaced one after another—love, fear, dread, and pain but also hope and nostalgia for something that I couldn't name —all these emotions flooded my being threatening to drown me alive in a stormy sea. Taking a deep breath, I forced myself back into reality, shying away from the connection threatening to destroy me.

"We need to get him out of here." Sissily pulled me out of my dread, already standing up and pulling River with her. "Now, Hazel."

I couldn't talk. I could only stare into his eyes trying to figure out the feelings I was experiencing.

"It's not going to be that easy, I'm afraid." Leviathan told her from the side where he stood observing our reaction to the bomb he so nonchalantly delivered. "How very interesting." He moved closer when he realized River was awake and looking at me.

"Well, unless you are planning on killing us, we are getting him out..." Sissily trailed off when she glanced down at River's face.

"You knew this was going to happen!" I demanded angrily, wiping away the tears that had gathered on my lashes with a fierce swipe of my hand.

"I had an inkling," River rasped, lifting himself off the ground in vain as his arm gave out. I lunged forward and caught him before he fell, but the regret on his face said it all. "But I wasn't sure," he added, his gaze pinning me to the spot.

Betrayal was a bitter pill to swallow, and I had no idea why I expected something else from him. He was Danika's pawn after all. No truth would be coming my way from Blackman, not even when it comes to his own wellbeing. It hurt more than it should've but just because he was a piece of work it didn't mean I had to be one too.

"We are taking him out of here." I told the demon not leaving any room for an argument.

"Why are you in such a hurry?" Grinning like the cat that ate the canary, Leviathan spun on his heels and strode toward the only door in the room. "Just a little bit longer and he will be all mine." With his hand curling around the handle, he cracked it open and glanced back at me. "I'll return when he is ready to swear fealty to me. Then we can talk."

"You fucker!" I screamed and jumped up to give chase, but I was too slow.

The door slammed shut and he disappeared from view before I took one step. Shrieking in anger, I pounded the walls with no luck of finding it until my fist throbbed in pain, the skin turning purple where it bruised.

"Leviathan, I swear to everything I hold dear if you don't let us get him out of here I'm going to bring down the wrath of my coven on your head." My voice bounced off of the tall ceiling and stone walls. "You hear me!" Screaming until my throat was raw did me no favors at all.

The fucker laughed.

"It's not worth losing your voice over." Sissily pointed out glumly. "He left us no exit for a reason. I doubt it was just so he can return and guide us to the surface."

"Since when did you become so pessimistic?" Eyeing her warily, I searched for any signs that Leviathan somehow switched her with that creature Charon tried to trick me with. "Normally you're a glass half full along with the voice of reason. I'm the gloom and doom one."

"I'm just tired." Wiping sweat from her forehead, she slid down the wall and tucked her knees to her chest pressing her face in them. "Do you know how long we've been here?"

"No." My short answer had her lifting her head so she could raise her eyebrow at me. "And I don't care how long it has been. It could be a day it could be a month. All I know is we are getting out of here." A yawn made my jaw crack loudly. "Now that you mentioned it, I do feel tired, too."

Alarm bells started going off in my head. Sissily was nodding off, her head was lolling to the side. River was breathing evenly, already fully back asleep. If I wasn't still upset by the confirmation from him that he knew he could change into a fallen here, I wouldn't have believed he was awake a little bit ago. It was Leviathan's doing. I had no doubts. It was so he could keep us docile until time was up for Blondie.

Well, not if I could help it.

Determined not to allow the demon to win, I tapped my face in rapid succession before doing it to Sissily, as well. She protested loudly, slapping my hands away but at least she was awake.

"Stop...slapping...me...you...asshole..." she kicked and even tried to bite me at one point. "Get...away...from...me."

"You need to get up." I said firmly, taking hold of Sissily's flailing arms and yanking her up. "Think, Sissily! Does this seem like you? It doesn't—it's that jerk making us feel this way. Don't let him win. Shake it off." I shook her shoulders hard, and she finally frowned at me as if it never occurred to her that she was acting out of character.

"Hit me," she whispered, leaning back slightly so I could see the pleading in her eyes.

So, I did.

There was no other option; I had to do something drastic to snap her out of it, so I did the only thing I could think of—I slapped her so hard that her head flew to the side and the elastic band holding her ponytail together flew off. Strands of blonde hair covered half of her face as she brought a hand up to rub at the stinging skin on her cheek.

"Snap out of it!" I hissed, my own anger boiling up again as tears started streaming down Sissily's cheeks.

"Holy crap! That hurt." Gasping, she gave me such a look of shock a stab of shame pierced my chest.

"You told me to hit you." I defended lamely, my face heating up in shame. "Sorry."

"I meant zap me with a bit of power to shake off whatever magic was cast on us, you jerk. Not for you to peel half of my face off." Rubbing her cheek, she glared at me. At least she wasn't falling asleep.

"Well, you shook it off, didn't you? See? Helpful." I pointed at my own chest. "Not so helpful." I pointed at her chest. "Who's the jerk now?"

"You are seriously mental." Sissily deadpanned, but her lips twitched at the corners.

"You say that like it's a bad thing." Bumping my shoulder on hers, I looked down at River who was sleeping the entire shit show away.

I wished we could trade places.

"We need to find a way out of here." Crouching, I touched the back of my fingers to his skin. It was clammy and cold to the touch, which sent my heart racing. "He seriously doesn't have much time. I don't think he deserves this fate, although I'm tempted to just leave him here because he didn't warn us of what could happen."

"He's here because he wanted to make sure we were safe." She kneeled on his other side and checked his pulse. "Well," her mouth twisted in a grimace. "To make sure you are safe. In their eyes, I'm just a convenience appointed to stay close to you. And I'm okay with that." She rushed to reassure me.

"I'm already feeling like shit girl, no need to lay it on thicker." Unaware of my own actions, I brushed a lock of hair from his forehead with a curled-up finger. When I realized what I did, my eyes snapped up to Sissily who was watching me with a sad face. "We have no other option but for me to use my magic and blast us out of here. It worked in the hallway to find this place. I don't see why it wouldn't work to get us out."

"It's not like we have anything to lose." She agreed with me, worry for River clouding her eyes. "I'll be ready to fry anything that dares to try and stop us after you make us an exit. Do it."

Jumping to my feet, I dusted off my pants and eyed the wall. Logically, if I slammed power into the spot where the door used to be before Leviathan hid it, it should appear for us again. That being said, nothing worked as it should in this cursed goddess forsaken realm. For all I knew a water buffalo would pop up and start belly dancing if I tried to find an exit.

"Any day now." Sissily encouraged very unhelpfully.

So, not helping right now girl." Shaking my hands off to get rid of the nerves I blew a nervous breath. "I have a bad feeling about this."

"Yeah, well if you don't do it, River will have no feeling

at all. So just blast the thing." Her hand sliced the air indicating I should cut the stone open.

With what? My sharp wit? Not that I would say that out loud. They counted on me, and I had to make sure they got out of this alive; and the same species as when they entered here.

With a deep breath, I held it and closed my eyes then called on my magic.

The voices started eagerly whispering their gibberish of nothings and I felt the power gathering in the center of my chest. Something was still telling me that I shouldn't be doing this, but what choice did I have. We had to get River out of the Underworld. No matter what happened I had to at least try. He was in this mess because of me. It was as sweet as it was infuriating.

I used those feelings to fuel my magic, and slapping both hands on the stone wall, I released it full force. It did nothing to the wall, but it sure paid me in kind for my idiocy; not. Life was much easier and less painful when I thought I was a dud. The impact of my magic against the stone threw me back on my ass hard enough I thought my tailbone broke. With a yelp, I curled on my side rubbing my ass to soothe the crippling pain.

You, okay?" Sissily rushed to my side and helped me stand up.

"That was dumb." Taking her offered hand, I glared at the untouched wall. "I feel like we are missing something. That should've opened a hole directly in front of my house. Look at it. It doesn't have a mark."

Sissily unleashed a torrent of flames, wind and even lightning bolts on it with the same luck I had. An unmarked stone mocked us from across the room. Finally, the archdemon took pity on us and his voice floated to my ears from all sides at once.

"I feel generous for some reason, Miss Byrne." His amusement was loud and clear in his tone. "I will give you an opportunity to prove you are worthy of your powers. If you do that, I will let you leave."

"All of us will leave, right?" I wanted to make sure in case he tried to trick me again.

"It could be arranged." He mused. "Do we have a deal?"

"Hazel, don't. I don't trust him." Sissily whispered under her breath but what choice did we have?

"Deal." I hissed, stewing from the helpless situation.

"Oh, how lovely." The demon crooned and four doors popped up in existence at once. "The moment you touch a door, all three of you will go through. Good luck."

"Oh fuck!" I was already reaching for one of them thinking I'd check what's behind it?

Chapter Fourteen

Water surrounded me from all sides. A dim light was blinking in and out of existence somewhere in the distance, but it was hard to tell if that was real or not. Leviathan's voice droned on in my head, repeating that both my companions would be sucked in with me the moment I touched a door. Which meant they were stuck in the water too, and I needed to find them before it was too late, and goddess forbid one of them drowned.

Strong currents pulled on my limbs as I tried my best to turn around and search for River and Sissily. Teeth grinding, it took everything in me not to open my mouth and suck in water, my screaming lungs demanding I supply them with oxygen without delay. If I knew being dunked in water was an option, I would've taken a deep breath before I found myself in the middle of whatever it was, a lake, an ocean…but I didn't. My heartbeat was drumming in my ears so loud it was fueling my panic more.

Shadows elongated at the corners of my vision, tormenting me with threats of something monstrous coming out of nowhere to snuff out my life. I had to find a way out so I could gulp much needed air before I drowned myself; so, pushing the fear aside, I decided the best way to go was up.

Legs kicking with all my strength, I forced my body to move faster than it wanted. The longer I surged upward, the darker the area around me became. A sinking suspicion that I was going in the wrong direction had me stopping, and as much as I couldn't afford it, I was treading in the water so I could get my bearings. Much to my dislike, it only confirmed that I was not alone. When suddenly on my left everything turned pitch black, and I caught a sight of a snake-like body slithering away. It was twice the size of the width of my body and trepidation filled me so suddenly I almost tried to breathe.

My chest started hurting and my vision started blurring, so I did the opposite of what my brain was telling me to do, and I started swimming down. With a last-ditch effort to reach the surface, I gave it everything I got. My two companions and I were about to die in this cursed place too. While I worried about them and did my best to find them, I bet they were doing the same.

Maybe not River, since he was not aware of what was going on.

Which meant he could already be dead.

Anxiety was riding my ass like it was a race horse and the finish line was in sight, so I redoubled my efforts. A few spells crossed my mind where I could form a protection bubble that would, or could possibly save my life, but I didn't have all the words. The water was tugging on my clothing and shoes slowing me down, and it was destroying my focus, too.

To my shock it was becoming lighter in the water

surrounding me, and I pushed myself, grasping at the liquid as if I was trying to dig myself out of a sink hole. There was no finesse in my kicks or strokes, just a bone deep desperation for survival. Just when I thought I was going to pass out, my head broke the surface of the water.

My intake of air was so loud it echoed for a good minute in my ears. Coughing and splattering, I ended up swallowing a lot of the disgusting water that resulted in me nearly coughing out a lung. But blessed oxygen was filling my deprived body, so I was crying out with sheer happiness. Somehow, I was sure that the end was near, and I was about to meet the goddess up close and personal.

"Sissily." The first attempt at calling out for her was pathetic at best. Not just that, but something wrapped around my ankle and tugged at my leg, so I ended up with a mouthful of water.

Hacking and flailing, I kicked angrily at whatever was trying to pull me under. Too exhausted to be afraid, I was either hoping to hurt it or make it angry enough to eat me and save me from my misery. Anything would do.

"River." My rasp was sad, raw, and filled with anguish. I was one hundred percent sure all three of us were going to die here. "Sissily." Treading water, I turned left and right seeing nothing but gray mist and churning water.

As I took a deep breath hoping to call out louder, the creature that took a liking to me wrapped around my right leg again and yanked me under the water. My lungs were placated with the supply of oxygen I provided them, unintentionally, during my previous struggle, so I was able to take a good look at my tormentor.

At that same second, I wished I hadn't.

No wonder they say ignorance is bliss.

The monster wasn't a snake as my mind so kindly

provided out of fear, initially. It was a mix between an octopus and a squid with twice the number of tentacles; it was wiggling them menacingly at my face. One of the said protrusions suddenly flicked out and slapped me so hard on the side of the face and neck I screamed underwater, emptying all the air from my lungs. Yeah, I knew it was a dumb thing to do the second I was done shrieking but that didn't fix my breathing problem.

I panicked that I was going to drown, so I started frantically kicking and reaching for the surface. If I had stayed calm, I would've handled it better I guess, but tell that to my monkey brain. My brain needed oxygen and it wanted it now. So, I flailed like an idiot for a while as the octo-squid thingy tugged me back every time I made an inch of progress.

What was Hell's obsession with kraken-like creatures anyway. It was beyond me.

The need to cry was in the back of my mind too, because at that point I was pretty sure there was a good chance that River was already dead. Fully awake, I nearly died a few times. There was no way he survived the changes his body was undergoing while he lay unconscious. At least, that was the thought processes I currently had. Why am I thinking this way? Is it the fact I had a monster trying to kill me, I swallowed a river, or that my anxiety is sky high because I am currently underwater fighting for my life?

My head finally broke the surface, and I sucked in a quick breath before I was pulled under. Renewed desperation raised my magic that was nowhere to be found while panic was clouding my thoughts and judgment. It was almost as if it was hiding while I was in the Underworld, and only making an appearance when it absolutely had too.

It should've been a hint, but who paid any attention to it?

I'll give you a hint. Not me.

Annoyingly, the octo-squid thought I was a toy, and kept tugging at me, jarring my teeth together when it jerked me through the water while tightening its hold on my feet. Angry, tired, and depressed since I was sure I lost Sissily and River, I reached with my hand and latched onto one of the swirling tentacles. I released all my pent-up anger and sadness.

I electrocuted the cursed thing.

The body of the creature lit up as if I zapped it with a lightning bolt. I could've sworn I saw the spine bone at the center of its head like a blob. That would've been great if I didn't do it to myself too; the water was a perfect conductor for the electric jolt. Teeth rattling, I was glued to the monster, both of us trembling from the force of the attack. Everything around me brightened, and through the seizure-like shaking I thought I saw two bodies floating in the distance ahead of me.

Octo-squid screeched so loud underwater that my ears popped, and warmth leaked from them. If I ended up alive but deaf from this ordeal, I was going to torture Leviathan one papercut at a time for at least a century. I didn't get rid of one shortcoming when I stopped being a dud, so I could end up with another. But that was a worry for another time because the damn creature apparently had teeth.

"Fuck!" I shouted as my head popped out of the water and I sucked in a much-needed breath. "Oh, shit, shit, shit." Kicking as fast as I could, I dared not think about how the monster was about to take a bite from one of my legs like it's a drumstick. "There is no meat on me fucker, go away. It's more like a chicken wing than a turkey leg." Or it could bite my Hoo-ha too, and I gasped in outrage at the thought of that.

Nasty water filled my mouth while I prattled nonsense, so I promptly clamped it shut. Stabbing my hand in the water and hopefully aiming it at the creature, I sent another attack with whatever my magic found suitable. I was prepared to electrocute myself again to save my vagina.

"Hazel." Sissily's voice was a balm to my soul.

Jerking my head up, I whipped it left and right searching for her. Her head was bobbing a few feet away behind me and she had her arm wrapped around River's chest. I nearly sank under the water from the relief I experienced at seeing them both alive.

"Careful there is an octo-squid below us." I shouted and started clawing at the water so I could reach them. "I zapped it," Spitting water out, I continued. "But that only pissed it off, I think."

"An octo-what?" She coughed but treaded the water toward me too. "Did you hit your head?"

A tentacle burst up between us, flopping angrily before sinking back down. Sissily screamed and reared back trying to stay out of its reach, but I had different plans. Now that I could see my bestie and River, all I wanted was to get us out of here. Leviathan said I needed to prove I was worthy. I was about to give him a show that would turn his hair gray.

"Hold on to your panties girl." I told Sissily and raised my arm above my head as high as I could, letting magic gather around my fingers. It hissed and spat like an angry cobra from the intensity.

"What are you doing?" Sissily gaped, her eyes became so wide they were going to pop out of her head. "You'll kill us all."

"We'll be fine." I pushed through clenched teeth.

I had no idea if we were going to be fine, but what choice did we have? Stay in the cursed water and wait for that octo-squid to munch on us? Or float until something else came to kill us before we drowned. Screw that.

"I'm about to turn this ocean or lake into a fish stew before I allow anything that is not a hot guy to eat our vaginas." I told Sissily firmly and her jaw dropped open as if she thought I had finally lost my mind.

Maybe I did.

With a shrug at her traumatized look, I jabbed my charged arm in the water and released the current of magic that was eager to do as much damage as it could. I hoped it would fry any creature in the water but leave the three of us safe. Unfortunately, River got a seizure at the same time, and his body was jerking and flopping in Sissily's hold. It lasted for a good minute or two before everything stopped.

Silence stretched between us; Sissily and I were staring at each other with wide eyes.

"Is he alive?" I had to know. I'd never forgive myself if I killed him.

"Umm," reaching for his throat, she closed her eyes for a second. "Yeah, he still has a pulse."

"His heart might explode too." River croaked and my heart skipped a beat. "You trying to kill me, Miss Byrne?"

"Always, Blackman." I choked out through unshed tears. Sissily was openly sobbing and clinging to him when she saw him awaken.

Any idea where we are?" Blondie asked, looking around in confusion.

"I think I saw a similar door to the one we entered but it was down." Sissily pointed toward the bottom of the ocean-lake.

"How sure are you?" I eyed her dubiously.

"I'm sure." She simply said watching me steadily.

"Okay, let's get out of here but hold onto me like your life depends on it. And don't let go of Blackman." In a couple of strokes, I was next to them and Sissily twisted her hand around my shirt. The wet fabric cut into my skin but that was good. I'd be able to notice if she lost her grip.

"I'm ready." River was preparing weakly to take a breath and hold it.

"Let's go." With a sharp intake of breath, I dived in taking both of them with me.

When we were under water, I turned to Sissily, and she pointed in the direction where she saw the door. Jaw clenched, I resisted the urge to go up for air one more time and kicked with everything in me in the direction she pointed. It felt like an eternity that we spent looking for it, and I almost gave up twice, but finally, I saw the door.

It was floating in the middle of the water with nothing to hold it in place. Eager to depart this place, I renewed my efforts, and to my shock, the closer I pushed us to the door, desperately begging the goddess to help me reach it, the further the exit seemed to be. Desperation and fatigue were fighting for supremacy inside me, but it was the loosening of Sissily's hold on my shirt that fired up my brain to think. Everything in the Underworld so far has been the opposite of what it appeared. And it was all meant to trick me. So, throwing caution to the wind instead of desperately pushing to reach the door, I started pulling away from it. I wanted nothing to do with the cursed door and prayed to be as far away from it as possible.

The door wiggled for a second and it darted at us with an incredible speed. I had no time to process what was happening before it was looming in my face and it sucked us in. We dropped to the stone floor of the chamber we left from, splattering, coughing and dripping water everywhere.

We made it." Sissily cried flopping on her back and starfishing it.

"We made it.' I agreed, checking quickly that River was still breathing. His intense gaze sent a jolt through me when our eyes met. Unaware of what I was doing, I started crawling toward him, and too late I noticed my pinky brushing against wood. River's eyes widened, but there was no point of a warning.

"Ah, fuck." Was all I had time to say before we were sucked into another door.

Fuck my life, indeed, as Sissily would say.

Chapter Fifteen

The good news is I was not dumped into the water again. That fact almost made me weep with joy. Great thing since I was sure that I would've drowned. My limbs felt heavy, and I was dead tired from everything that happened.

The bad news was that I was free falling. Yup, the cursed door dumped my ass in the sky.

I was not a goddess. Damn pigeon!

Clouds were zooming by me, and my still wet hair was slapping me punishingly on my face, maybe even breaking skin. I had never seen anything so white in my whole life. The clouds were so bright that they hurt my eyes. It was like being caught in the middle of a snow storm without sunglasses. My hair wrapped around my face like a blindfold as well, the slipping strands going in and out of my mouth, clogging my nostrils and making it hard to breathe through them. It was like something was whipping me across my nose and cheeks, and tears started streaming from the corners of my eyes. One thought I clung to however was that at least River was awake when I touched the door, and he had wings.

Surely, he would save Sissily and I.

The thick scent of sulfur and rust was overwhelming my senses. The smell was so potent that I gagged on it. Fear did its own thing to my brain, and in that fright, I believe that I'm plummeting to my death, so I kept flailing. That only made things worse because my body was flipping ass overhead, and the speed with which I was going down kept increasing. For the longest time, I thought that I could hear Sissily screaming until I realized it was me that was shrieking loud enough to give the Mazzikin a run for their money.

I clamped my mouth shut.

The sky continued to spin around me, and my stomach was filling my mouth with acid from the rising nausea as I was getting dizzy. To prevent vomit from spilling all over myself, I closed my eyes and breathed through my nose. This reminded me of the one-year Sissily was obsessed with roller coasters, and I spent a whole summer in Cider Point lining up for every ride until it closed every day. They called it the Roller Coaster Capital of the World. I called it a metal death trap waiting to happen.

This reminded me of that summer.

I hated it then, and I only did it to make my best friend happy.

I also hate it now.

My ass was still flipping over my head, and I had to focus on my breath so I could think clearly. Caught up in my air acrobatics, I also managed to notice some brown and green patches down below, before I reached the ground. That told me those were the spots where my skull would burst like a melon.

I wanted to prevent that from happening.

The cry of a large bird came just as I managed to take control of my panic. It messed up my equilibrium immediately and I cursed under my breath, my eyes flying open. It sent my heart into overdrive, jackhammering my ribs with a vengeance which made me want to puke more.

A shadow fell over me, saving my poor sight from the blinding brightness, but when I saw what was circling above me, I would've been happy to go blind any day. Who needed to see? Not this girl, to be sure. Especially when there was a harpy retracting and contracting her talons within reach of my head. Wings the color of steel spread behind her bare torso as she twisted and turned eyeing me curiously. Her three breasts swayed with the movement bringing my attention to them and I gagged when I saw the hairs covering the nipples. I had no idea what any of my ancestors had done but this was some karmic shit right there. No one has that much bad luck, I would've bet my life on it.

She lifted her head and screamed at the skies when she heard the noise of disgust I made. When her red eyes locked on mine the intensity of her rage froze the blood in my veins. It made me wonder why I thought the octo-squid was scary. Compared to the harpy it was all but cuddly as far as I was concerned.

I shrieked so loud I think I ripped my voice cords.

The harpy was taken by surprise, and so was I to be honest, and she jerked back from me spreading her wings wide to stop her movement. I saw it as the blessing that was presented to me, and as fast as I could, I slapped my arms parallel with my body. Clutching my pants, I flipped around and pointed my head downward like I've seen skydivers do on some of the videos I watched on TikTok.

And they say social media can't save your life.

I'd beg to differ.

My body shot like an arrow toward the ever-widening ground. I could make out the tips of trees and the sharp points of rocks on top of the mountains already. It sent a new wave of dread through me, but better I burst like a ripe grape than be eaten alive by a harpy. I bet that bitch was going to peck my eyes out first. I could tell by the way she glared at me when I screamed.

A shout of panic was ripped from my mouth that hurt my throat when talons wrapped around my hips, and I was plucked from the air like a fly. With nothing else to do but refusing to go down without a fight, I started wiggling, kicking, and scratching at any part of the harpy I could reach. She was taken by surprise at my pathetic attempt at freedom, so she opened her claws and dropped me.

Head over ass I tumbled through the air, gratitude filling me with warmth until I remembered that I was going to die anyway when I splattered on the ground. The lesser of two evils, but still. On the bright side, if the harpy was busy with me, Sissily and River would either live or splatter like grapes in peace. No one will be stringing their intestines along and eating them like licorice. Unfortunately, I must've surprised the creature enough to send it packing because the brightness returned to sear my retinas and I continued to tumble through the sky with the wind whistling in my ears.

In the distance something broke the monotony of the clouds, like a dark stain on the white background. Squinting at it with my heart in my throat, I prayed it wasn't the harpy deciding to return and munch on me like I was an overcooked pretzel. No one likes those, but who knows if a demon has a taste. Not long ago, one tried to eat my Prada shirt. You can never be sure with Hell spawn. Vampires were a safer option for survival, I would bet my life on it.

The stain kept increasing even when I glued my arms to my sides and tried to speed up my meeting with death. In the meantime, I decided that if the harpy reached me, I'd just zap her with magic. See how she likes being fried. That would teach her a lesson I thought to myself deliriously, to avoid hyperventilating in fear.

"Hazel." It took me a second to realize it was Sissily's voice again.

How was it that she always found me when I ended up dealing with cursed monsters in each door I opened? I needed to catch a break one of these days. Speaking of which, recalling the videos I'd seen of skydivers, I tried to slow down my descent by spreading my arms and legs wide in an attempt to hug the air. It worked for a second, but I turned a bit too much to the side and I pitched forward again with a cry of despair. In my flailing, I saw a bird shooting right at me, and in between the panic, Sissily screeching something, and my own spiral of death, I paid no attention to what it was. All I wanted was just for it to go away and stay away from Sissily and I.

I zapped it.

My magic hit it head on, sending it flipping backwards, and a sigh was ripped from my chest. Nothing was going to eat us today, I told myself firmly. Until I heard what Sissily was shouting from the top of her lungs.

"You almost killed River you idiot." My best friend was bellowing from a foot or two below me. "Are you blind?"

"What?" Freaked out, I twisted and turned so I could find the bird thingy I threw magic at. To my horror, white wings streamed limply behind a large muscular body that was swirling toward the ground. "Oh no. River." I gasped in horror.

Instead of saving him, I actually killed him. The blood curdled in my veins. Without giving my brain a chance to think or panic, I aimed my body toward the falling Blackman and straightening my arms I shot like an arrow at him. If I could reach him, maybe I can do something to slow his fall. Or wake him up and he can actually save us all.

The closer I got, while Sissily kept shouting things from behind me, the more I realized his skin was almost gray. Unsure if it was the realm doing it to him or my magic that I hit him with, I pushed it aside and focused on getting my hands on him. Who would've thought I'd be eager to wrap my arms around Blackman. Yet here we were.

I barreled into him with the force of a freight train, our bodies slapping into each other with a resounding smack that hurt my ears. At that point, I was so tired from all the fighting, swimming and flailing, that my fingers had no strength to tighten around his arms. He slipped from my grip like water, and I lost contact.

"Eggs bound em." Sissily's words came out in almost a whisper.

"What?' I shouted and cringed from the pain in my throat. "Eggs? It's not a bird, it's Blackman." To make my point clear, I pointed at him a few times. Couldn't she see? I mean he was a pigeon but it's impossible not to recognize River. Even as a supernatural he had a perfection about him that was hard to match.

"Eggs bound em." She pointed too and I frowned when she started to kick at the air.

Was she frogging in the air? It took me a long moment

of staring, and Sissily humping and thrusting her pelvis at the air to understand what she was saying.

"Oh!" I wanted to slap my forehead, but I couldn't from the pressure of the air whistling around me. "You want me to wrap my legs around him. Smart thinking." I told her, but I doubt she heard me. I couldn't hear me either. The important thing was I understood what she said, and she was right. If I could wrap my legs around him, I could definitely hold him to me.

Angling my body to the best of my ability, I made a second attempt at grabbing a hold of him. Sissily, by that point, learned my trick too, so she was doing the same. Both of us zipped and zagged around him, thankfully avoiding each other, and not cracking our skulls in the process.

After the fourth attempt, I finally snatched River's falling body and latched onto him with my arms and legs. Locking my ankles at the small of his back, I dug my heels in his rounded buttocks and plastered myself to him. A second later Sissily slammed into us and latched on too.

Now we were spiraling down to our death in a bundle of three.

"Do something." She yelled at me, ever so helpful.

"You do something." I snapped out of desperation, more like anger, but I was already craning my neck to see something that would inspire me.

"Arrowing down was genius by the way." She kept talking and hiccupping, which told me how nervous and stressed out she was. It also reminded me that I have seen situations like this, so I wracked my brain to think about how to slow down our fall. I almost cried from relief when an idea struck me.

Releasing the death grip, I had on River's shoulders, I slid my hand down his arm until I tangled my fingers through his. Lifting our hands, I showed Sissily and pointed for her to do the same with his other hand. She looked at me strangely, but did it anyway, thank Hecate. I reached for her free hand with my other one and waited until she laced her fingers with mine. Then I released my locked ankles from around Blackman's hips and my body was flung up at the same time as Sissily's who was doing everything I was doing. The moment we were only linked by our hands our descent stopped and we started floating up.

"Hopefully the door is floating around here somewhere." I said more to myself than her.

"Actually, it's not down here." Sissily shouted, and I whipped my head straight to look at her.

Her chin jerked up and she raised her eyes toward the space above us. I followed her line-of-sight, anger gathering at the center of my chest. Sure, as hell the door was looming above us, but we had to aim our bodies to reach it and not miss it completely. To make matters worse, the cursed harpy was back. She circled us from afar once but was coming closer.

"What in Hecate's name is that?" Sissily asked alarmed, the distress evident on her face.

"A demon, courtesy of Leviathan, I'm sure." The twist of my mouth told her how annoyed I was with it.

"I can hit it with magic, but I'll have to let go." My bestie shouted.

"I'll hold onto your forearm," I yelled back. "I won't let go."

With a nod, we forced our fingers to unlatch, and I walked my hand from her palm to her forearm where I dug my nails into her skin, so my hold didn't slip. She didn't complain, just clenched her jaw, and lifted her head up and zeroed in on the harpy.

"She's coming this way." My shout hopefully stayed between us, and the demon couldn't hear it. "Wait till the last minute."

Sissily nodded to tell me she heard me, just a quick jerk of her head. I held my breath and kept glancing at Blackman hoping to see him awake. I was not sure I could live with the idea that he was dead because of me, despite all the back and forth between us. I was mean to him because if I allowed myself, I would care too much about him. And when he hurt me, I would never recover from it.

It'll kill me.

"Almost." Sissily said, pulling me out of my internal conflict.

"I'm ready."

The harpy spiraled in the air, and instead of coming right at us, she pulled her body back and stretched her talons at River's wings. The claws grabbed a hold of the white feathers and yanked him hard to try and dislodge him from us. Sissily screamed in anger, while I tightened my fingers on his painfully, just so I didn't release my hold. It threw us in a breakneck spin through the air. I almost let go of both of them. Luckily, I didn't, and Sissily managed to release a stream of fire at the harpy while missing Blackman's wings.

Screeching, the demon reared back and flew away shedding burning feathers in her wake. Her screams were echoing around us, but I was more focused on the door above our heads than the harpy. If we reached it, the demon would be of no concern.

"We need to spin." I yelled, so Sissily could hear me. "It's the only way to hit it."

She looked up once before nodding at me. Adjusting our hold now that she didn't need to use her magic, we swung our legs to start the swirl. All three of our bodies turned into a circle, moving faster with each new round as if we were catapulted from a spinner. Holding my breath and recalling the water, when I was trying to reach the door, I prayed not to touch this one either.

We hit it full force, hard enough I was left dazed on my knees on the stone floor of the chamber. River and Sissily hit the ground too next to me, but this time I didn't release their hands.

Who said I don't learn my lessons?

Lesson number 15: *If at first you don't succeed, try again. And again. If that doesn't work, kill anything that stands in your way.*

"We made it." Sissily breathed. "Don't move so you don't touch anything." She rushed to warn me.

I nodded. And then my foot kicked at something hard, and we were sucked through another door.

Seriously!

Chapter Sixteen

My knees and hands buried themselves in soft moist soil, twigs and rocks digging through the fabric of my pants and breaking the skin of my palms. Immediately, my head snapped up and I searched for Sissily and River because I knew I didn't release my hold on either of them before we were pulled through the next door.

I was fed up with the bullshit!

This had nothing to do with me proving my worth and everything to do with wasting time until there was no saving, River. Leviathan was buying time until the transformation was over. I knew it as well as I knew my own name. On the bright side, Sissily and River both landed on the forest floor next to me. I didn't have to worry about if I will find them.

This ominous woodland is cloaked in perpetual shadow, shrouded in an eerie mist that swirls around ancient, gnarled trees that seem to be twisted by the malevolence that pervades the air. Goosebumps covered me from head to toe and I shivered as I looked around.

Staying silent, I helped Sissily and River up while holding Blackman between us so we could support his weight. We start moving forward.

As we venture deeper into the accursed forest, I notice the trees taking on unnatural shapes, their branches resembling skeletal claws reaching out for unsuspecting prey, stretching in our direction. Shrinking back, I tuck myself closer to River and pull Sissily the same way, as well. The ground is carpeted with thick, thorny vines that seem to writhe and move of their own accord, eagerly ensnaring those who dare to tread too close.

The silence is broken by the haunting cries of nocturnal creatures—werewolves howl at the blood red moon, their eyes gleaming with a savage hunger for flesh through the foliage everywhere I turn. When I catch a sight of them my heart skips a beat. These are no packs like I had ever seen. These were some sort of distorted versions, specifically made for Leviathan's pleasure. I was sure of it, as we roamed around this place. Their fur was matted and dark, and their elongated fangs glistened with fresh blood. These cursed beings are not mere shifters, but hybrids of a demon and wolf, bound to a distorted lycanthropic curse under the malevolent influence of the Underworld's sinister energy.

Among the trees, demonic figures lurked in the shadows, too, their forms ever-changing and elusive. Horned creatures with glowing eyes and sharp claws wait to torment any hapless souls who wander too far from the safety of the path. They are the denizens of the dark, embodiments of malice who feed on fear and despair. How I knew this I had no clue, but I refused to question it. Keeping Sissily and River close, I pushed forward hoping beyond hope we would see the door soon. I was tired of the games, tired of fighting.

I was simply drained.

The air was heavy with a foul stench that was clogging my chest—a mixture of decay, sulfur, and the unmistakable scent of maleficent magic was flooding my nostrils and filling me with dread. Strange wisps of unnatural light flickered around through the branches, hinting at the presence of mischievous spirits that delight in leading travelers astray.

Aware of the ethereal wails that echoed through the forest, I had a feeling they were tormented spirits of those who lost their way and fell prey to the forest's stillness. Their anguished cries filled the space with a haunting reminder of the price one pays for venturing into this cursed domain.

"Am I the only one that has dramatic thoughts that don't sound like me, or do you guys have the same?" Sissily leaned over to glance at me across Blackman. "It's almost as if I have a twilight narrator guiding me through the damn forest."

Now that she mentioned it, I shook my head and dispelled the horrible thoughts. Heavy fog was crowding my head, building a tension headache behind my eyes.

"Good catch." I mumbled rubbing at my gritty eyelids that felt like sandpaper. "I'm so tired right now I don't pay attention to anything that's not trying to kill me immediately."

"Same." Sissily's chirp was followed by a mournful howl too close for my liking.

"How are you doing, River?" Tucking my shoulder deeper under his arm I peeked at him.

"I have been better but I'm alive." His voice was raspy and low like it took everything in him to say those words. "You should leave me here. It'll be safer for you."

My snort sent a cloud of birds flying into the night sky.

"Not happening, Blackman." I told him. "Keep moving or I'll zap your pigeon ass!"

"What she said!" Sissily jostled him to tuck her shoulder under his, that is the best way to support him.

River chuckled and squeezed me affectionately. A lump formed in my throat.

Another howl split the night, and I tripped over some rock buried in a bunch of leaves. Instead of me holding River up, he tightened his arm around me, so I don't face-plant in the dirt. My mumbled apology had him tucking me in closer to his body and sharing his body heat; what little he had left in him. Fear raked my insides when I noticed how cold his skin had become. All the emotions from earlier, or was it a month ago, who knows how long it has been, came rushing in threatening to double me over.

"It's going to be okay." He mumbled.

I knew Sissily could hear him too, but with the night surrounding us, and his arm around me, it was almost an intimate whisper. Swallowing thickly, I didn't say a word, I just pressed my mouth tight and stayed alert. Something was going to come at us at any moment I could feel it.

We started walking faster, but that didn't make much of a difference with all of the obstacles we were facing. Trying to dodge roots, mud puddles, and fallen branches became tedious work that left us all exhausted by the time we reached an opening in the trees. We arrived at an edge of a clearing where an old building stood with its walls covered in ivy and moss. The structure was dilapidated looking, as if it hadn't seen use for years. It seemed like no one had stepped foot on this property for centuries, and that made me uneasy.

"We should take shelter." Sissily rushed to crack open the door and to check if the building was empty.

River and I stood outside until she poked her head out and motioned for us to enter. The dust and dirt smacked me in the face the moment I stepped foot inside, but it was better than nothing. Whatever came our way, it would be easier to defend ourselves from the old house for sure. Heavy wooden beams supported a thatched roof over a sturdy stone foundation. Broken pieces of long forgotten furniture were sprinkled everywhere I looked.

"River needs to rest." I said as I guided him to a corner and helped him slide down. "I'm going to look around and see if the door is anywhere nearby. When I find it, I'll come get you."

"I think we should stick together." Sissily glanced from River to me, nervously twisting her fingers. Every second word was followed with a hiccup too. It spoke volumes about what state she was in.

Not just me, they were being drained too, and all this because I couldn't stay put where I was told. I had to do things my way and run into danger to find out what? What exactly did I think Leviathan was going to do? Spill all his secrets to me? Now time was nearly up, and River was going to be stuck in Hell under Leviathan's thumb no doubt. Sissily could get hurt and is probably traumatized for life, and as for me?

I'd always had a screw loose. Short of dying, I had no idea what was going to be different about me. Before Sissily convinced me to stay with them, I spun on my heel and rushed out of the old house.

Anger and guilt made me run for a while, blindly through the dark forest, the glowing eyes of creatures and demons following in my wake. I didn't care about any of it. My magic was a living thing inside of me the longer I let the rage build, so I was hoping any of them would dare to test my patience. In my rush to escape my thoughts, I tripped over a root sticking out of a tree and pitched forward, sliding a few feet on my stomach over the forest floor.

Screaming in anger, I punched and kicked at the ground and leaves until I had no strength to breathe, much less anything else. The slow clapping penetrated the fog in my brain after a while. Spitting a bunch of leaves out that filled my mouth I raised up on my knees to face the monster that applauded my misery.

Dressed in dress pants, a button down that had its buttons opened to the top of his abs, and his hair perfectly brushed was Leviathan. Leaning his shoulder on a tree, he watched me with a glint in his eyes, his vertical pupils expanding and retracting in excitement. Each slow clap was like a nail in my temples, and if I had any strength left, I would've gotten up and punched him in his smug face.

"Impressive." He murmured, not blinking in case he missed a twitch of a muscle on my face.

I glared at him.

"You don't believe me, that I'm impressed?"

"I don't care what you are."

"You should." Watching me down his nose, he frowned at my dismissal. "You carry my blood in your pathetic body."

"Feel free to remove yourself from it if you can." Plopping on my ass I blew out a breath. "You won't hear me complaining."

"Ungrateful vermin." The demon spat at me, but I was so beyond caring that I started laughing.

"Am I worthy now you jerk?" Snorting and giggling, I dropped on my back and stared at the tree tops. "Let Sissily and River go. You can do whatever you want with me."

"That's not how this works, you need to go through all the doors."

"No."

"What?"

"You heard me, I said no." I was tired to my bone marrow, and I wasn't going to play anymore of his games. "I'm done."

"Stand up and continue the test."

I blinked at him lazily.

"I will release the Nephilim and the witch if you do one more test." He changed tactics. I should've negotiated from the beginning.

"You let them go, and I'll think about it." Something else occurred to me, and I sat up. "Who betrayed Alex? You said you bought the loyalty of his pack."

"That's what you care to know?" Cocking his head to the side, he watched me as if I was the unknown creature in the forest.

"Yes. If you tell me that and release my friends, I'll do your stupid test."

Leviathan studied me for so long I thought he would tell me to get lost and unleash a bunch of demons on my arrogant and rude ass. Instead, he started chuckling, and after he was done laughing at me, he watched me with a proud grin.

"It was one of the she wolves that warms River Blackman's bed that was easy to buy. All I needed was for her to pour the potion which would lure the Mazzikin to pack lands and protect them from being exorcised. That way I knew they would bring you to me."

Danika's voice sounded in my head *'What you are looking for is looking for you.'*

Not once did she say that ever since this craziness

started. My grandmother knows more than she tells, and her lies need to come to an end eventually. I also wanted to laugh that River is getting laid and I'm the one paying the price. I bet it was that blonde that barged into my room who betrayed Alex. At least now I knew to tell Sissily to warn him after I convinced Leviathan to let them leave the Underworld. I couldn't even be angry at River. Good for him and all the orgasms he received.

He's not dumb like me.

"So, do we have a deal?" I asked the demon watching him steadily.

"I have a better proposition."

"Of course, you do." I drawled and jumped when a twig cracked behind me.

I shouldn't have worried because Sissily with River draped over her stepped into the clearing where I was still on the ground in the bed of leaves.

"Now that everyone is here," Leviathan smiled smugly. "I will tell you the task."

"I can't wait." Rubbing my face, I shook my head. There was no winning with the cursed demon. He was going to have the last say no matter what.

"There are two doors." He started and I groaned so long and loud he glared daggers at me.

"I told you no more doors." I snapped.

"These are different." With the patience of a saint, I took a breath and smoothed his unbuttoned shirt. "There are two doors and two guardians of them."

Two horned demons stepped out of the shadows resembling minotaur's just as two doors popped into existence. Sissily hurried to join me and kneeled next to me on the forest floor dragging River with her. She took my hand and squeezed reassuringly without saying a word. I had to swallow a lump.

"You can ask only one question. And they can give only one answer each. One of them always tells the truth, the other one always tells a lie." Triumph was written all over Leviathan's face. "If you guess which door is the exit to your world, all three of you can leave. If you guess the wrong one, the two of them will immediately die and you will stay here until you give birth to your first child conceived with me."

"I beg your fucking pardon?" Outraged, I stared daggers at him. "This is your way of telling me you want to screw me. Get the fuck out of here you pervert."

"That's my offer. Take it or leave it." With a shrug he folded his arms across his chest and watched me unblinking.

"Don't do it, Hazel." Sissily whispered, digging her nails into my hand. "We can pass the trials no matter what he throws at us."

Leviathan watched me as if frozen in place, and my heart stopped for a few beats before hammering against my ribs.

"Give me your word." I told him through a fist tightening my throat.

"Hazel…" River rasped, and I had to look at him.

You are almost out of time, River. I can't live with myself if you get stuck here." His eyes bore into mine, but I was almost out of courage. I had to do this. "By the way your fuck buddy betrayed Alex. You should tell him that when you see him. Because one way or another, you are leaving the Underworld even if I have to kill Leviathan to get you out."

"Ask which door leads to our home and I will cast a spell

to discover the correct answer." Sissily told me, determination loud and clear in her tone.

"Witch magic does not work on the guardians." Leviathan shrugged unconcerned.

"There must be another way." I mumbled, still watching the archdemon. His vertical irises were glittering in excitement.

My fingers were brushing against the fallen leaves absently when I thought I heard something. Slowing down the movement, I focused on the voice I thought I heard and was shocked to find the roots had intelligence. They eagerly shared their secrets with me through my affinity for Fae magic. It took everything in me not to laugh in Leviathan's face.

"I'm ready to ask my question." I told him and his smirk grew so wide it nearly split his face in two.

"Go ahead." He rubbed his hands together in glee.

"Hazel, maybe we can think on it a little?" Sissily tugged on my arm, uncertainty coloring her tone.

"Nah I'm good." Taking a breath to build suspense, I looked at the two cows on steroids. "What answer will the other guardian give if I ask which door will lead me home?"

It was comical to see the shock on Leviathans face when both guardians pointed at the same door.

The wrong door.

The one telling the truth pointed at the wrong door. The one telling the lie pointed at the door that was a lie since the truthful guardian would've pointed at the other one. It was ingenious, if you asked me, and I was forever grateful to the roots for their help. I sent them warmth and love through my fingers without the demon seeing. He was still gaping when the air shimmered and the correct door sucked us in and spat us out in front of my coven doors.

Sissily was shrieking out of joy and hugging River and I so tightly, I couldn't breathe. I was about to tell her to let go when a voice cut through my best friend's cheers.

"Hazel Byrne." Danika's voice cut like a whip.

"I thought we left Hell." I groaned at Sissily, and River snorted while returning to his normal color. With a deep breath, bracing for a tongue lashing, I stood up on my feet and turned to face my grandmother. Jutting my chin up, I met her emerald gaze with a stubbornness only a Byrne witch can have.

"I thought you were dead." She barked at me.

"Witch, please." Cocking my hip, I smirked at her. "Have you met me?"

Next in the Chronicles of Forbidden Witchery Series

vinci-books.com/paybackisawitch

There's screwing up a spell… and then there's *my* level of catastrophe.

I've got the ambition of a Ferrari but the skill of a Go-Kart. When my magic goes sideways, there's no undo button—just demons, lies, and a one-way trip to Hell. But once I claw my way out?
Payback is a witch.

Turn the page for a free preview…

Payback is a Witch: Chapter One

Lesson 16: *If you can't beat them, join them, although old habits die hard.*

I didn't follow anyone, by principle.

I learned this one on the day as I stood at the bottom of the steps leading toward the great double doors of my coven building, more so than any other time of my life. I couldn't say why to save my life, and it truly pissed me off.

My eyes traveled slowly from the bottom of the steps, over the monstrosity of the building, until they settled on the very top of the glass dome, and I swallowed thickly the fear that tried to claw its way up my throat. While I was too busy self-loathing and doing my best not to die, they rebuilt the damage I caused to the structure, not once but twice.

Just as I was rounding the corner at the edge of the last bookshelf, my shoulder bumped into a line of stacked books protruding from it. It made me stagger, and the grimoire I had in my hands dropped on the floor with a heavy thud. That was followed by another smack when the damn book, which jabbed me in the arm, hit the ground too, falling on the spine, and it flopped open somewhere in the middle. An invisible breeze skirted across my skin, and goosebumps covered my arms. My heart jammed in my windpipe, and I flipped around, searching for some asshole with air magic trying to pull a prank on me.

But no one was in the library other than me.

Dread pooled in my stomach, and I really didn't want to be in the damn room anymore. The first traces of dawn were peeking through the tall windows, casting purples and pinks over the wooden shelves and leather tomes. What little light was poking through the brightening sky pierced the liquid in the jars, giving all the eyeballs, fingers, and such a menacing vibe. I had every intention of snatching the grimoire and hightailing it out of there, but when I bent at the waist to grab it, the text on the opened book got my attention. It was a siren song overtaking my mind.

I was powerless to resist it.

A horn blared somewhere in the distance, dragging me out of whatever rabbit hole my damaged brain cells were pulling me into, and I realized my fists were balled so tightly that my nails were cutting through the skin of my wet palms.

"You are seriously pathetic," I muttered to myself as I wiped my sweaty palms off my pants in disgust. "Witches don't get PTSD. Get your shit together, girl."

The pentagram on the side of my finger tingled at that, reminding me that my life was no longer the same. I was no longer that same person every member of the coven gossiped about and whispered insults behind her back. Well, they still did that, but for entirely different reasons now.

I was no longer a dud.

I was the monster all of them feared.

Even Danika thought twice before squaring off with me these days.

Yet again. Here I was....

A scared little mouse with shaky knees, too afraid to kick in the damn doors and walk in like I owned the place.

I was seriously pathetic and should be put down immediately—preferably in my designer clothing. I would turn in my grave if I ended up in the afterlife dressed in polyester.

A shiver skirted up my spine.

Instead of keeling over right then and there, with each step I counted the slow exhales of my breaths until I was certain that my heartbeats no longer resembled a galloping racehorse while making sure that no one saw the ridiculous display of weakness. Stupid, I knew, but as I said, old habits died hard. Deep down I was still the old Hazel. The one that hid her inadequacy behind a smart mouth, lots of bravado and a legendary sense of fashion if I could say so myself. My designer shoes and the leather wrapped around me could attest to that last statement even to a blind person.

On one side though, a very hidden -don't even tell myself where it was- space, I liked the new Hazel better. She was everything I ever wanted to be while growing up thinking I had zero gifts. Powerful supernaturals cowered in front of the force of her magic. It was who I prayed to the Goddess to make me when I was growing up. What I never expected was for the people I cared about to be near constant threat of dying because of it. I wanted magic so bad so I could protect them better, not get them killed faster. For that reason, that part of the new me I disliked with a passion as much as I loved it.

Which was the main reason I now stood in front of the closed doors of my coven, staring up at the three red keys marking it as a tribute to Hecate. None of the skeleton keys were crooked, and they all looked brand new—as if the Goddess herself was pointing out to me that no matter how powerful I was, she could erase me from existence without a second thought. Like I never existed. Deep down, I was sure that I was working on borrowed time and had to do something before it was too late.

Something had to change, and I knew just the person to talk to about it. The problem I had was I had to swallow my pride along with the newly formed lump in my throat, to actually walk in and get it over with.

Danika didn't bite. I mean, what could she do now? She couldn't kill me if she tried.

I should've asked Sissily to come with me, but I thought she could use a day off from my drama. Good thing too because she never would've let me forget it when the double doors unexpectedly opened and I jumped almost a foot in the air. Luckily, I clamped my mouth shut and only a tiny squeak escaped me, hopefully low enough that the person barging through the damn entrance didn't hear it.

The male that walked out was someone I'd seen in passing a lot around the coven, but I couldn't remember his name to save my life.

"Hecate help me, Miss Byrne." The middle-aged witch gasped, pressing a flat palm at the center of his chest. "You scared me."

My glare reminded him that on the best of days I was not a friendly person for that type of a conversation, so he rushed to backtrack in the same breath. "I just didn't expect anyone to be standing there, that's all. Not that *you* are scary." My glower deepened more at that, and he gulped, going as far as taking a step back and bumping the slowly closing door which made him jump a little to the side instead, as if physical difference would save him from my anger.

My magic reared its ugly head with those thoughts, churning at the center of my chest like a cobra waiting to strike. What was worse, was the fact that I felt justified in attacking him according to the emotions filling my head. And all that from a simple, accidental bump in passing.

Who was I? What in the goddess's name was happening to me?

I despised bullies. I was *not* a bully.

Fear from the monster I was becoming overshadowed anything my powers could artificially produce inside my head, so I shook off the daze which was forcing its way to the surface. As much as I loved Danika, despite all the skeletons coming out of the closet and everything she'd done, I never wanted to become like her in that sense. I was an asshole, not an evil bitch. Still, I had a reputation to uphold that would hopefully keep people away from me. I never wanted to be a monster, but approachable I certainly was not.

"I could try harder if I'm not scary enough like this." Dust could've puffed out of my lips from the dryness of my tone as I cocked a hip and slapped my hand on it.

"I simply meant I didn't expect anyone to be anywhere near the coven at this hour, Miss Byrne." The male attempted to mold himself to one side of the door and mumbled almost to himself while color was draining from his face with each word. "It is the middle of the day."

"You are here," I told him reasonably; you'd think we were discussing the weather.

"I suppose you are correct." With a nervous chuckle that sounded more like a wheeze he slumped on the partially opened door, and I watched with rapt interest how a drop of sweat rolled down one side of his face.

"Doing what exactly?" My eyes narrowed and zoomed in like a hawk on the male for a totally different reason now.

"I beg your pardon?"

"You are here in the middle of the day when no one is around, doing what exactly that makes you so jumpy?" Speaking slowly and deliberately, I folded my arms across my chest and waited. When he said nothing for at least five seconds, my shoe started tapping and broke through the tense silence.

I'd learned that one from Sissily. It was proven to be an unnerving tactic when someone was trying to hide something. At least with me it was. Almost like a hot poker to my brain with each tap every time my friend did it.

"But...but...but..." the male stuttered, rearing his head up, straightening and unfolding like a constipated flamingo. Blush started spreading up, pinkening his neck within seconds from his anger at my interrogation.

See how much I cared about his outrage.

"But, but, but... What, sir?" Stabbing a French manicured finger at his rapidly reddening face, I squinted at him. "It's a simple question. Answer it!"

"If you are accusing me of some nefarious reasons for being inside this building, Miss Byrne, I will have no other choice but to bring this up with your grandmother." Squaring his shoulders, the so far meek-appearing male stuck his nose up so he could look down it at me. "I am a respected member of this coven and will not allow myself to be questioned like a common crook. Not even by you." Yanking on his collared shirt unnecessarily, he puffed out his chest.

"That still didn't answer my question," I deadpanned, as the right side of my mouth twisted in annoyance. Would it be such a terrible thing if I socked him in the head, I thought to myself?

Another horn blaring, this one much closer than the one before, destroyed the built-up tension I had created hoping to make the male talk. Not that I had a feeling he was doing something wrong. But I'd learned the hard way that these days I couldn't trust anyone or anything. Check first, trust later.

Look at me all grown up.

I was ready to pat myself on the back when the male hunched down and gave me all of two seconds before he tackled me out of nowhere. All the air was pushed out of my chest with a loud grunt when my back hit the pavement hard enough I heard one of my ribs crack. The back of my skull followed with a resounding smack on the patterned marble and black roses bloomed in front of my eyes while nausea churned in my gut.

"Motherfuc…" I wheezed a second before a fist was jabbed in my side, forcing me to involuntarily curl up so I could protect my organs. The asshole was doing his damn best to relocate my kidneys, I would've asked if he was a nephrologist if I had any breath left in me.

A few more knees and knuckles connected with parts of my body before I realized the male had no intention of stopping his assault. This was not a simple reaction to me insulting him by asking what he was doing in the building in the middle of the day as he claimed. Oh, no. As was my luck lately, I'd stumbled on some clusterfuck I would've rather avoided. Unfortunately, the douche didn't give me the option to refuse.

Sharp pain was spreading from my left shoulder all the way down to my pinky toe which was made worse when I twisted to that side in hopes to avoid another punch to my ribs. As a reward I received a fist in my left boob and saw stars spinning when my eyes rolled to the back of my head.

A scream was ripped out of me at that, but it sounded more like a yell of outrage than one caused by pain. My legs managed to wrap around his, and I hooked the heels of my shoes as best I could so he couldn't shake me off. With a sharp twist of my hips, I successfully turned us around so that he was now under me and I was straddling his thighs. The owlish look he gave me when I grinned at him through crazy strands of my messed-up hair made every punch and kick I received worth it.

"You didn't think I'd let you have all the fun the whole time, did you?" I told him when he started buckling in an attempt to get away. Laughing, I rammed my fist in his cheekbone, widening my smile when I felt it crunch under my knuckles. "How boring, darling. I prefer to be the one on top."

Holding him firmly on the ground, I returned the favor by rearranging his organs until he stopped buckling and trying to escape. When he stopped moving, so did I, and I sat fully on the back of my legs, breathing loud enough to be heard all the way to New York. My knuckles were shredded and I could feel the blood that sprayed me in the face trickle down my chin. I tried to wipe it with my forearm then grimaced when it smudged all over the sleeve of my shirt. There was no way blood was coming off the angora sweater I was wearing. I'd managed to ruin yet another shirt in the cursed coven.

"Hazel?" Ace's voice coming from the steps made me close my eyes and beg the universe for patience. "What in the world are you doing?" The soles of his combat boots thumped a soothing rhythm as he ran toward me.

"If I told you it wasn't my fault and he started it, would you believe me?" I asked with my eyes still closed.

"A fight not your fault?" The snort coming out of him as his shadow fell over me, darkening the midday sun, spoke volumes. "No."

"I didn't think so." On a heavy sigh, I pushed myself up and stood to face him.

"You're bleeding," Ace snarled, all humor leaving his features as he stepped too close for my comfort and reached for my face.

"Yeah, well." Jerking away from his fingers I sidestepped to put distance between us in case he made a grab for me. "You should've seen the other guy." He looked unimpressed at my joke, his wolf flashing briefly in his irises, but I had other things to worry about instead of Ace's feelings. "You gonna help me carry him inside or you don't want to dirty your clothes? I need to know what he was doing here that made it worth it to attack me when I caught him leaving."

Not Ace but a predator watched me contemplatively for a long moment through narrowed eyes. Stubbornly, I kept my gaze locked on the shifter as best I could since one of my eyes was slowly swelling up. Without a word, he bent over and snatched the passed-out male from the ground, unceremoniously tossing him over his shoulder. Stunned, I watched his back retreating for a long second before I snapped out of it and rushed to catch up with him.

"Such a gentleman." I wheezed, holding my side and hating my pretty shoes at that moment. I could bet my newfound magic that my compliment did not impress the wolf.

Grab your copy…
vinci-books.com/paybackisawitch

About the Author

Maya Daniels, USA Today Bestselling and multi-award-winning supernatural suspense author, is a fun-loving woman with many talents.

She traveled the world, gaining life experiences that helped her career as an investigative journalist, as well as her storytelling. Maya writes compelling tales of magic, mythical creatures, loyalty, and life-changing friendships with snarky female characters—much like herself.

Her travels have taken her to Europe, Africa, Asia, Australia, and America. Born with her feet in motion, she currently resides in Ohio, spinning her next epic story that you will not want to put down.

Her biggest 'sins' are her love of chocolate and coffee—through an IV drip! One to never sit still, Maya practices Reiki healing, different types of martial arts, reads about the arcane, talks to furry creatures more than humans, picks up a sledgehammer for home improvement, and travels with her fated mate, seeking her own adventures.

www.ingramcontent.com/pod-product-compliance
Ingram Content Group UK Ltd.
Pitfield, Milton Keynes, MK11 3LW, UK
UKHW040035130426
469799UK00003B/114